Mills & Boon
Best Seller Romance

A chance to read and collect some of the best-loved novels from Mills & Boon—the world's largest publisher of romantic fiction.

Every month, four titles by favourite Mills & Boon authors will be re-published in the *Best Seller Romance* series.

A list of other titles in the *Best Seller Romance* series can be found at the end of this book.

Anne Hampson

ETERNAL SUMMER

MILLS & BOON LIMITED
LONDON · TORONTO

First published 1969
Australian copyright 1981
Philippine copyright 1981
This edition 1981

© Harlequin Enterprises B. V. 1969

ISBN 0 263 73653 9

Set in Linotype Baskerville 10 on 11 pt.

Made and printed in Great Britain by Richard Clay (The Chaucer Press) Ltd, Bungay, Suffolk

CHAPTER ONE

SHE glanced through the window and her heart lurched. The man beside her sat reading his newspaper and she tried to fix her attention on the unfamiliar letters. He spoke curtly, telling her to relax.

'I can't.'

She hadn't realized she was clutching her seat belt until his hands uncurled her fingers. He slid the belt off her knee; her handkerchief lay there with its clumsily embroidered initial.

'How do you come to have a Greek name?'

'As you know, my father loved Greece.' His face was close to hers, dark and sinister. 'And the people.'

Her eyes were drawn to the window again. The coastline now, and the sea. Clouds gathered swiftly.

'Think of something else.' He returned to his newspaper, and after casting him a reproachful glance she looked round. Everyone was acting naturally, laughing, ordering drinks. Through the opposite window she saw they were enveloped in cloud, sun-tinted; the plane seemed to hover, scarcely moving. She managed to sit back, glancing at the clock.

Could it be only a few hours since they had sat waiting – waiting to see which of her sisters Mr. Loukas would take?

The twins had never looked more beautiful, or so elegantly groomed, and as she glanced from one to the other Marika had wondered how Mr. Loukas could possibly make a choice.

Would he prefer Carol, with her long golden hair and vivid blue eyes? Or would he choose Susan? Susan's fair hair was a cluster of curls framing a tiny heart-shaped face; she had an adorable smile and the poise and figure of a model.

Speculating on the question of whom she would miss the most, Marika felt quite shocked to find that she did not care which of her sisters went to live with Mr. Loukas and his family in the remote village of Delphi in Greece, for she appeared to have little in common with either of them. For one thing, she was four years younger than they, and for another, the twins seemed to enjoy all those pastimes which Marika abhorred. They belonged to a smart set of merry young people who frequented country clubs and inns, who threw all-night parties and had expensive tastes in holidays and clothes. Consequently they spent all they earned and more besides. So for Marika and her mother it was a hand-to-mouth existence that had reached a climax just over three weeks ago. Heavily in debt, Mrs. Vaughan had written to Mr. Loukas imploring his help. His reply had caused much excitement and speculation in the Vaughan household, for he had offered to relieve the strain on the family's finances by giving one of the girls a home with him – 'For a period not exceeding two years'. This had seemed mystifying to Marika, and David, she recollected, had been most sceptical about the whole affair, asserting that Mr. Loukas must have some ulterior motive for his offer. Why, for instance, should he insist on coming to England and making his own choice? Were he genuine it would not matter to him which of the girls went over to live in Greece. And why bother to have one of them at all? It would be far simpler to pay off the debts, or increase the allowance.

However, as Marika herself was not involved, and as neither her mother nor the twins appeared to find anything amiss with the proposal, it was eagerly accepted.

Returning her attention to the twins for a moment, Marika wondered if they had given serious thought to what was in store for the one chosen. True, Delphi was gay with tourists for quite a long period of the year, but

6

the winter must be exceedingly bleak and lonely.

Her thoughts were interrupted as the door opened and her mother entered, with a rustle of silk, and more than a hint of perfume. After bestowing a glance of satisfaction and pride on the twins, sitting demurely on the couch, she was plainly disconcerted at seeing Marika standing there by the open window.

'Weren't you going out, dear?' she inquired anxiously and Marika had to smile, not merely at her mother's lack of tact, but at the incongruity of her own attire.

Her jeans were frayed at the bottoms and patched at the knees; the collar of her shirt was also frayed, and the sleeves rolled up merely to hide the holes in the elbows. Several of her sandal straps had come adrift at various times and Marika had stitched them with different coloured threads.

'Don't worry,' she laughed. 'I'll make myself scarce when I see him coming—' She broke off, her eyes dancing as she heard the unexpected but welcome whistle from the direction of the paddock. 'In fact, I'm off right now!' and like a flash she was gone, much to her mother's relief.

She ran lightly down the drive, crossed the footpath, and sped on to the gate where David sat waiting.

'You've come!' she exclaimed gaily, tucking her hand into his. 'You said you wouldn't be able to make it. Didn't you get the job at the filling station, after all?'

'Part-time only. I'm having to share it with another student. He's on duty now; I relieve him at five.'

They wandered down the lane, their fingers entwined, and Marika wondered whether he were disappointed about the job. He had hoped to earn enough to go on holiday with a friend later on, towards the end of the vacation.

'Has the great benefactor arrived yet?' They had reached the stile; Marika bounded nimbly over it, then stepped aside, waiting for David to follow.

7

'No, he's not due till three.' She glanced at David's watch. 'He should be arriving about now.' Perhaps he had arrived; perhaps his decision was already made. 'One of the twins is going to be terribly disappointed.' She fell into step beside him and his hand found hers again.

'That's life.' He sounded troubled, she thought, and hoped he hadn't been working too hard. 'We have to learn to accept disappointments – they're usually only temporary.'

An odd note in his voice caused her to glance up sharply, but he turned away, avoiding her eyes, and Marika recollected that something quite intangible in his last letter had caused her some slight misgiving.

They had been brought up in the same village. David had rescued her once, from the school's bully. From then on she had regarded him in the light of a hero, and had tagged along in his wake whenever the opportunity presented itself. As they grew older Marika was not at all sure what she wanted from David, but he had given her affection, and always at the back of her mind there dwelt a vague anticipation of a future both pleasant and secure.

Two terms at college had wrought a subtle change in him and she felt oddly disturbed.

'What's he like?' David asked, guiding her towards a field path.

'Tall and dark and grim, judging by the photographs Daddy used to show us – and quite old.'

'Old?' He seemed surprised. 'I hadn't that impression, not from the things you've said at various times. How old?'

'Oh. . . .' She wrinkled her brow. 'I'm not very good at judging ages, especially from photographs; besides, they were taken years ago. He'll be more than thirty by now, I should think.'

'You call that old! You're such a baby, Rik!'

'You keep on calling me that,' she retorted, on a

8

plaintive note, and then, tossing her head, 'In fact, I don't know what you see in me at all!'

'Nor do I,' he returned with the old, boyish grin she knew and loved. 'It isn't your looks – and those clothes! You're like a street urchin.' He laughed then, and Marika laughed with him, happy that he could still tease her in the old familiar way.

'I'm not really ugly, though, am I?'

'Ugly? What gave you that idea?'

'You once said it was Cinderella in reverse. Two beautiful sisters and one ugly one.'

'I never did!' he emphatically denied, and then, 'If I did, I was only joking. Here, let me have a look, there might have been an improvement since last time I was home.' Stopping in the path, he touched her face, noting the high cheekbones, and the tracery of blue veins at her temples, showing through the pale transparency of her skin. 'You have all the basic necessities,' he stated with a new-found knowledge. 'Widely-spaced eyes – and those lashes! Hmm ... the bud is coming along nicely; the warmth of love will one day bring forth the flower.'

One day ... Marika swallowed a little lump in her throat. What was he trying to convey? She said flatly,

'Can we go into the forest?'

'It will be wet underfoot.' David frowned his objection.

'I know, but it doesn't matter. I want the – peace.'

'Very well.' Because his conscience troubled him he pretended not to understand the reason for her dejection. 'Is all this business of Mr. Loukas getting you down?'

She shook her head.

'I'm not involved.'

'It's an odd set-up, a Greek looking after your money.'

'Father invested in his business.'

'It's still odd; he's so young to have been your father's friend. He'd only be about twenty-five when your father died.'

Marika remained silent. His voice held a hint of

curiosity which, for some obscure reason, she felt unwilling to satisfy.

It was, in fact, old Mr. Loukas who had been her father's friend. They had met while on holiday over thirty years ago, and although their ways had parted after only three weeks' acquaintance, they had corresponded regularly, and when Mr. Loukas bought his first hotel Marika's father invested his small savings in it. They now lived on the dividend from this investment.

When old Mr. Loukas became ill with an incurable disease and was confined to his bed, his two sons took over the management of the business and, consequently, the Vaughan finances. The elder son was later killed in a road accident, leaving Nickolas in control of the business, which now consisted of two hotels in Athens, and others on several of the islands, including Crete, Rhodes and Corfu.

These details of the Loukas fortunes had been given to Marika by Elaine, the sister of a school friend who had recently returned from Athens, after having taught for three years at the American school there. She had made friends with some people at Delphi who had been acquainted with the Loukases for many years. Elaine had also passed on information regarding their private life, but this had been of no interest to Marika, and she had not even bothered to pass it on to her family.

'You're quiet, Rik.' David's voice sounded faintly anxious. 'What are you thinking?'

'Nothing important.' It was the first time, she reflected, that she did not wish to share with him all her innermost thoughts.

The corn grew low and green on one side of the path, and from the hedgerow on the other side the scent of May blossom hung in the air. High above them a lark sang for sheer joy, loud and sweet and clear. In spite of herself Marika's spirits rose; she flung back her head and her dark eyes met his in a challenge.

'I'll race you to the forest,' she cried. 'Count ten for my start!'

He watched her go, a brooding expression on his face. Lithe, yet too thin, he mused, just as she was immature and yet so often wise. Earnest and intense, yet too shy and timid for the kind of fun he was just beginning to enjoy. She looked round, giving him permission to start, and with a sigh he followed, catching her up as they reached the barbed wire fence. He held it aloft for her to pass underneath, and she in turn held it up for him. After strolling a little way into the forest they sat down on a newly-felled tree. The stillness around them was broken only by the rustle of leaves and the occasional call of a bird.

'It makes you feel . . . good. Clean and sort of – holy.' Her eyes held wonderment, like a child straining to understand. Her smile was sweet and faintly sad. 'Do you feel it, David?'

He did not, she knew. He bit his lip, feeling a surge of anger against her because of his conscience. Yet, paradoxically, he wished he were older and had the patience to wait for her. But nineteen was the age of excitement and experiment; he had no time to linger, waiting for little girls to grow up.

Seeing that he would not answer, Marika changed the subject to less personal matters.

'I wonder if he's decided yet. Will it be Susan, do you think?'

'You're not a bit envious, are you?' He eyed her curiously, glad of the diversion. 'Wouldn't you like to go to Greece?'

She thought about this.

'Father used to talk such a lot about it,' she murmured, almost to herself. 'I think it must be a very beautiful country.'

'Yet you're not envious?' he said again.

'Of course not. Would you be?'

'Frankly, I would. You should have stayed; he might have chosen you.'

She winced, and said in a bleak little voice,

'You would not care if I went away – so far away?'

'Not if you were to benefit. I'd miss you for a while, I suppose, but we don't see much of each other now that I'm at college. And you'd have a wonderful life, among all that wealth. Think of the sunshine, too – and no tax on all the things you want most to buy! Where did you say he lives? Somewhere near Athens?'

'Delphi; it's a hundred miles from Athens, so Elaine says.'

'Delphi of the Oracle – Sanctuary of the sun god, Apollo.' A rather disgruntled note entered his voice. 'Lucky blighter, whichever one he chooses!' He glanced at Marika again. 'Yes, you should have stayed – you might have had a chance.'

Her lip quivered, but she turned away so that he should not see. Greece was like a place at the other end of the earth . . . and David didn't care if she went there.

Clouds began to gather, hiding the sun, and the forest took on a sombre, eerie aspect. With a little sigh she rose, and David, unable to prevaricate any longer, said impatiently,

'Marika, you don't love me.'

'I know my own mind,' she said in a low voice, hurt even by the way he used her name. He did that on the rare occasions when they had quarrelled.

David shook his head emphatically.

'You'll have dozens of boys before you settle for one, and I shall have lots of girls. That's how it is, and that's how it ought to be.'

She stared at him in wonderment.

'You think it's right to have – dozens?'

He made no answer and, blinking away the hurtful pricks behind her eyes, she lifted her head proudly. She said it was time they were going, and his relief could be felt. The way back seemed long, so long, and Marika felt her heart would break. She wouldn't cry, not yet; all the way home she chatted, asking about his college work, and when they came to say good-bye she waved gaily and forced herself to smile.

Immediately he became lost to sight her footsteps flagged. Mr. Lowe passed in his car and waved to her. That only increased her misery, for he didn't want her, either. She'd been working in his nursery since she left school last year, but his son had wished to enter the business. There wasn't enough work for two of them and Marika had been out of a job now for almost a month.

On turning the corner she saw a taxi standing outside the house, with the driver waiting patiently at the wheel.

So Mr. Loukas had not yet gone.

As there was no necessity for her to meet him, she entered the house quietly, crossed the tiny hall, and had begun to mount the stairs when her mother appeared from the sitting-room, her whole demeanour one of urgency.

'Marika, where have you been all this time! Come in here at once; Mr. Loukas wishes to see you – oh, dear, those clothes; what will he think!'

'Me?' Frowning, Marika obeyed, though with unconcealed reluctance.

Apparently something had gone wrong. Carol, tight-lipped with anger, sat upright on the couch, while Susan, an expression of bitter disappointment marring her lovely face, left the room as Marika entered, slamming the door behind her. Marika's frown deepened. Could it be that he wanted neither girl? – that he had broken his promise? If so, it was a most wicked thing to do.

He stood with his back to the empty fireplace, hands deep in his pockets, his height dominating the room. Marika noticed the tensed muscles of his neck and the chin thrust firmly forward. The flint-like expression and taut lips accentuated the arrogant lines of his dark

13

features, and she was reminded of a picture she had seen of a Greek god, chiselled in stone. Cold, forbidding . . . and yet compelling.

Aware of his eyes upon her, she felt that every single thing about her was taken in in one sweeping look of surprise, of distaste and – could it be disappointment? His gaze travelled from her toes, not too clean after her walk in the forest, to her head. The wind had taken the shine from her hair; it fell untidily on to her shoulders. Although conscious of her unkempt appearance, she did not feel unduly perturbed by it. Under his prolonged unsmiling stare she was stripped, then dressed again, and after that there was a slight clearing of his brow before he said,

'Well, miss, now that you have at last favoured me with your presence, perhaps you will tell me why you weren't here, with your sisters, awaiting my arrival!' His English was excellent, but his tones were clipped, and almost menacingly quiet.

Marika could only stare. Was this how the Greeks spoke to their women? Some eastern men had a superior status, she knew; perhaps the Greeks were among them. Aware that he waited wrathfully for a reply, she spread her hands in a simple, self-deprecating gesture.

'I didn't think you would need me.' The slight stress on the last word did not escape him, and his eyes flickered oddly, but his tone did not change.

'Your mother informs me that you read my letter?'

'Yes.'

'You understood it?'

'Y-yes.'

'Perhaps you can tell me its contents?'

Marika stirred uncomfortably, embarrassed at being the centre of interest.

'It was written to Mother, and said that you were coming over to take one of her daughters back with you to Greece.'

14

'Exactly. And are you not one of Mrs. Vaughan's daughters?' He eyed her with stern inquiry and she inclined her head.

'Marika did not mean any disrespect, Mr. Loukas,' her mother put in, to Marika's intense relief. 'It was just that she thought – we all thought – that you would prefer one of the older girls.'

He ignored that.

'Why,' he said softly, his eyes still on Marika, 'do you think I sent the money for each one of you to obtain a passport?' Then he added, on an anxious but menacing note, 'I hope you have one?'

'Yes.' Her heart began to beat faster; she had not supposed, when she obtained the passport, that she would be called upon to use it.

'I'm relieved. When I give instructions I expect them to be followed. My instructions were that you should all be here when I arrived.'

Her face became hotter and hotter. She had never received much attention from her family, but neither had she been subjected to any form of humiliation. The experience was new, and she found herself hating this arrogant foreigner with a black venom.

'As you have wasted a considerable amount of my time,' he went on, glancing at his watch, 'I cannot allow you more than half an hour in which to change and pack. We have a long journey ahead of us.'

Speechless for one astounded moment, Marika put a finger to her breast and stammered,

'M-me!'

He nodded. Apparently a refusal was the last thing he expected.

'But, Mr. Loukas, one of the others would suit you much better—' Mrs. Vaughan began, when she was curtly interrupted.

'We have already gone into this. The others will not suit me at all. Marika is my choice.'

15

Wonderment, mingled with incredulity, spread slowly over her face. 'Marika is my choice.' He actually preferred her! For the first time in her life she had not been out-shone by her glittering sisters, and some vague exultation of which she felt half ashamed flooded her whole being. She forgot her hatred of a few moments ago, for this was flattery. It went to her head like a potent drug, and although her lips framed a polite refusal the words just would not come.

'Marika is a mere child, not yet eighteen,' her mother persisted. 'It would not be right for me to let her go with you. What would people think?'

The glance he gave Mrs. Vaughan made her daughter tremble in her shoes.

'Madam, are you implying that Marika would not be safe in my care?'

'Oh, no—'

'For your information, she will be far better protected than she is here. In my family young girls are not allowed to run wild unchaperoned. My cousin defers to my authority in this, and Marika will be expected to do the same!'

'How unutterably dull!' interposed Carol, and swept from the room.

'My letter to you included certain information about my family,' he went on, ignoring the interruption, 'but perhaps your memory needs refreshing.' But he directed his next words to Marika. 'You will have as your companion my cousin, Pitsa. She is Greek, but speaks English and is about your age. She is an orphan and has lived with us since she was twelve. You will like her, I am sure, and become good friends.' He went on to mention Hilary, his sister-in-law, who was English, and then there was his grandmother, who lived close by, and who preferred to be called Souphoula. 'A tyrant, I must confess, but if she takes to you you will have found a staunch and sincere friend. My father lives with us, but does not leave

16

his bed.' He turned again to Mrs. Vaughan. 'Before Marika came in I promised that, should I decide to take her, I would settle these debts of yours. This I am now willing to do.'

'But you also said that taking one of the girls would help us generally. Taking Marika will scarcely help us at—' She broke off in confusion. 'I mean—'

'You mean,' he cut in, his eyes narrowing perceptively, 'that Marika does not cost you very much.'

Marika gasped at his outspokenness. The man was positively rude!

Mrs. Vaughan admitted the truth of his statement, though she went on to add that it was Marika's own fault if she did not have the same needs as the others.

'We need not go into that,' he said curtly. 'I'll tell you what I'll do. In addition to clearing off these debts, I will personally increase your allowance.'

Personally? Marika wondered if that meant he didn't have complete control of the business. However, she dismissed that, though her thoughts remained on the matter of the allowance. He was so anxious for her to go with him that he would increase the allowance in addition to clearing off the debts. So David had been right; his offer had not stemmed from generosity. Clearly there was some specific reason for his wanting one of the girls to live with him – for wanting *her* to live with him. Surely her mother would see through it . . . but her heart sank as she noticed the gleam in her eyes at the mention of an increased allowance.

'Well, in that case, it's all right with me. Marika, you'd better go and get ready.'

Marika stared unbelievingly for a moment. Did her mother really think she would go with this stranger? True, for a brief moment she had basked in his flattery, but at no time had she seriously thought of going away with him.

'I'm not going,' she said quietly.

'You—?' Her mother gasped in disbelief. 'Of course you're going! Don't you realize how lucky you are? Your sisters would give anything to be in your shoes. Now come along; I'll help you.'

'I'm not going,' Marika said again, her face gradually draining of colour. 'No one can make me – I won't go, Mother, I won't!'

'Marika, you selfish girl! How can you refuse! Don't you care about any of us?'

White as a sheet now, Marika made no reply. Nickolas said, quietly,

'Madam, may I have a few minutes alone with your daughter?' His words were a command; after a flustered hesitation Mrs. Vaughan thankfully left the room.

He waited until the door had closed, then spoke with slow deliberation.

'Your mother has no money invested in my business.'

The heavy ticking of the wall clock was the only sound in the threatening silence that followed his words. Even though their full significance had not penetrated, Marika's heart raced, thudding madly against her ribs.

'We receive our cheque every month. My father put money into the firm, long ago. . . .'

'He withdrew his investment before he died.' His voice was pitiless, his meaning now quite clear.

'You sent us money – for nothing?'

'After your father died, your mother, believing the money to be still invested, wrote to my father. Realizing her straits, he made her an allowance. She remains in ignorance regarding the investment.'

'But why should you help us? It's five years since Daddy died.'

'The Greeks take their friendships seriously,' he said, and then, 'The business was later taken over by my brother and myself; we continued to pay your mother. Last year, after my brother was killed in an accident, I assumed ... control. The payments continued because my father wished it, but the decision is entirely mine. I can stop the allowance just whenever I please. I trust I make myself clear?' There was a cruel, relentless quality about him that seemed almost inhuman; Marika felt trapped, looking round in wild desperation as if to seek some means of escape. Her mouth trembled piteously. She wanted her mother ... David ... her sisters. Who would help her? She knew she was alone, and all hope fled as, for one fleeting moment, she held his merciless gaze before glancing away to hide her despair. What this man wanted he would have, not just on this occasion, but always. Marika had never been so sure of anything in her life.

'If I don't go with you my mother and sisters will have nothing?'

'Nothing.' He replied without hesitation, yet Marika sensed his next words were spoken in defence of his conduct. 'My father has only a short time to live — two years at most, but we think it will be considerably less. I will go to any lengths to ensure his peace of mind.'

'Your father?' Old Mr. Loukas who had been so good to them, and of whom her father spoke so highly. She recalled again David's assertion that Mr. Loukas had some specific reason for his offer; he had hinted darkly at all that was sinister. The Greeks were a hot-blooded, unpredictable race. One could not trust them. 'You want something of me?' she asked at last.

Sighing impatiently, he glanced again at his watch.

'I intended explaining on the journey,' he said. 'But perhaps there will be time.' He paused. 'If we miss our plane we shall have to stay overnight in London, that's all.' And he began to tell her, in his quiet, clipped tones, exactly what he wanted of her, and when he had finished Marika's heart was beating almost normally and the colour had returned to her cheeks. For his request was not so unreasonable, after all, considering the price he was willing to pay should it be granted.

'And that is all I shall have to do? I must assume the role of your fiancée until your father's death?'

'That is correct. It will give him happiness while he lives and tranquillity of mind at – at the end.' His voice became oddly tremulous for a man with such vigorous personal character and Marika's head jerked up in surprise. But she saw no change in his expression, could detect no sign that any warmth of feeling lay hidden beneath that cold exterior.

'If I do agree, you will pay Mother's cheque – indefinitely, you said?'

'I shall pay it for the rest of her life.'

'That is ... very generous of you,' she murmured, and then fell silent, watching him through brooding eyes as he moved with slight impatience as though tired of standing. The lowering sun cast shadows into the room and across his taut features. She frowned and glanced away to the drive where daffodils splashed their colour among the weeds. Was it only two hours since she had quickened to David's call? – had sped in happiness to his side, glad to be there, if only for a little while? David did not want her any more. He had found someone else – perhaps someone who was pretty. Turning from the window, she again examined this dark stranger, and her eyes were sad – sad, yet oddly grateful, too, as she said in gentle, childish tones,

'If that's all you wanted, one of my sisters would have done just as well. Why did you choose me?'

For the first time she saw a hint of a smile touch the hard outline of his mouth.

'You happen to be – my father's kind of girl,' he told her drily, and Marika once more spread her hands in a gesture of deprecation mingled with surprise.

'You mean your father would wish you to marry a girl like me!'

He nodded briefly.

'You sisters are too much like Hilary. As long as I am

presenting my fiancée, she might as well be someone he will consider suitable. You are the exact opposite of my sister-in-law.'

He had skimmed lightly over Hilary's character, but Marika, filling in the gaps in his brief narrative with what she had heard from Elaine, felt sure that it was Hilary's interest in other men that had caused the quarrel which had lead Andreas, her husband, to rush out of the house and drive the car so recklessly along the dangerous mountain road. Old Mr. Loukas had not spoken to Hilary since that day, for he blamed her for the accident. He had continued to fret about it and dwell on it until, for no apparent reason – or so Nickolas asserted – he became obsessed with the idea that Hilary now had designs on Nickolas, and that she would one day destroy him as she had destroyed his brother. Nickolas had not said so, but Marika gained the impression that Mr. Loukas had actually accused his son of being too friendly with Andreas's widow. As denials on the part of Nickolas were ineffective in dispelling his father's illusions he decided that the only remedy was to produce as his fiancée the kind of girl whom his father would wish him to marry. She would live in the house, so as to be on hand if ever reassurance became necessary. This, Marika felt, would be quite often, for according to Nickolas the long hours in bed gave him time to think up 'all sorts of odd notions', and she surmised these were almost always concerned with Nickolas and Hilary.

Marika, examining her own position, had to admit that she was neither wanted nor needed by anyone here, and as everything appeared to be over between her and David it did not seem to matter very much where she lived, or with whom. She held the power to make someone happy, to bring peace of mind to an old man who lived a long way off in a strange land of temples and gods. She knew her father would have wished her to go, to repay in some measure his friend's generosity over the allowance.

Despite the fact that she really had no alternative, Marika felt she was not, after all, being coerced into acceptance of this man's offer.

She began to wonder, for a moment, if there could be any foundation for the old man's fears regarding Hilary and his son, then decided it was not her concern and dismissed it from her mind to dwell fleetingly on the other people with whom she would live. All Greek except Hilary. Life would be strange at first, and yet she knew no qualms as she made up her mind. There was one thing, though, about which she must be sure.

'I don't know anything of the rules – the codes of your people regarding engagements,' she began, almost willing his face to soften, for speech was difficult under that cold and distant stare. But his features remained taut and she went on, rather timidly, 'There would not be anything binding in the engagement? – no danger of your being able to force me into—' She broke off, her colour rising as she endeavoured to re-phrase the question. 'You would never want to marry me?'

She might have insulted him, the way his glance swept over her in arrogant surprise.

'There is no – danger, as you term it, of my wanting to marry you.' His tones held contempt and Marika felt ashamed of her clothes, wishing she had changed. 'But make no mistake, you *will* be my fiancée. Unless you live the part you'll give yourself away. I warn you, my father is very astute, and, as I have said, I will go to any lengths to ensure his happiness.'

Somewhere in those words lay a hidden threat, but he gave her no time to analyse them. Taking her acceptance for granted, he reminded her of the time, and of the delay already caused by his having to wait for her to put in an appearance. Marika found herself inviting him to sit down, and promising she would be ready just as quickly as she could.

'Shall I tell Mother?' she asked, turning at the door.

'If you wish,' he said after a small hesitation. 'I cannot see her changing her mind.'

As Nickolas expected, they missed the flight he had intended to take, but managed to obtain seats on the plane leaving the following morning.

The airport terrified her, but her companion did not seem to notice. Certainly he was not in the least concerned about her fears. He carried two suitcases, Marika's, and his own smaller one. Marika carried a large cardboard box, on the lid of which was printed the name of a well-known multiple store.

'I s-suppose it must be s-safe – with all these people flying,' she commented, in a trembling little voice. It amazed her that everyone could appear so calm and untroubled.

Nickolas stopped and glanced around.

'There's a powder room over there,' he said at length. 'Go and change.'

'Change – here?'

'And what you have on you can leave behind.'

'You mean – leave my best dress and coat in the – in there?'

'I'll get rid of this luggage, and I think we have time for coffee.' He told her where to find him, adding, 'Now hurry, and don't get lost.' He strode away with the suitcases; she stood blinking after him for a moment, then turned and made her way in the direction he had indicated.

The habit of years could not be broken so easily; she folded her clothes with care and put them in the box, securing the lid with the string. Then she took a look at herself in the mirror. Considering Nickolas had chosen the entire outfit, even to the shoes, gloves and bag, in about fifteen minutes, she thought it suited her very well.

She found him without difficulty; her clothes gave her a touch of confidence and she smiled, inviting some comment on her appearance.

'What,' he frowningly inquired, 'are you carrying that empty box about with you for?'

'This?' Marika stood uncertainly by the table, conscious of the stout little man close by, his coffee cup poised half way to his mouth, his attention arrested. 'It isn't empty.'

'Not empty?'

'My other clothes are in it. You see, they're quite good really. . . .'

'I told you to leave them behind.' His tones were lowered, but sufficiently penetrating. 'Now do as I bid you.'

'It's such a shame—'

'Marika,' he interrupted, ignoring the curious, expectant gaze of the interested spectator who now seemed to be trying to determine their relationship, 'get rid of it!'

'Yes, Mr. Loukas.' She sped away, with a sudden desire to giggle as she visualized someone finding the box.

CHAPTER TWO

THEY were still enveloped in cloud. For the last hour Nickolas had been absorbed in his paper, silent and withdrawn. They had a meal, and towards the end of it his manner became less rigid and he began to talk about his father. Finally, he again stressed the need for caution, reminding her that from now on she must remember to call him Nickolas.

'It will be difficult at first,' she said uneasily, 'because I don't know you very well.'

'Then you had better begin practising,' he advised. 'Should you make a slip all will be ruined.'

'I know,' she agreed, still with the same uneasiness. 'I hope I won't make a slip.'

'I hope so too – for both our sakes,' and, leaving her to reflect on that cryptic remark, he again lapsed into silence.

His car was at the airport and, the customs formalities over, they were soon on their way, following the coast at first with the islands of Salamis and Aegina to their left, rising from a sea of dazzling blue. Soon they were heading north into a landscape of rugged, majestic splendour that belongs to Greece alone. They climbed, sometimes steeply, sometimes gently; they entered valleys and crossed wide plains; they rolled through bare and arid land, parched by a merciless sun. Marika could only gasp, often audibly, at the sheer wonder of it all as the changing vistas unfolded in slow procession before her spellbound gaze.

Nickolas drove in silence, his eyes on the road ahead; Marika wondered if to him this long journey was tedious and tiring and she welcomed his decision to stop at Levadia for refreshment. They drank Turkish coffee and iced water, but were soon on their way again, climbing steeply into the heady mountains. The greens and browns and yellows folded darkly into the mountain slopes as the sun began to set.

And then, looming ahead, dominating the landscape in all its splendid majesty, rose the mighty Parnassus, rugged, gaunt, towering to the sky.

Marika felt numbed, stupefied by the devastating beauty of the scene. Here was a place remote from man — and even nature; this was the mysterious realm of the gods, though the gods all slumbered now. An ache gripped her throat, the ache that comes when the burden of sheer ecstasy no longer can be borne. She whispered in a voice husky with emotion,

'It makes you want to cry.'

To her surprise he slowed down to a crawl, seeking for a place to stop. Having found one, he brought the car to a standstill and they both got out. Marika's eyes sought the road, the writhing, perilous ascent along which Nickolas had brought her ... to the very brink of Paradise.

She stirred restlessly, conscious of a profound sense of isolation. Nickolas alone seemed real as they stood, side by side, poised above the drifting sands of time, where past and future held no substance, and dreams, desires and vain ambition melted into unreality.

Nickolas broke the silence; he looked darker now and almost evil in that unearthly violet half-light which follows in the wake of a lowering sun.

'If you think this beautiful, wait until you see Delphi itself.'

Delphi ... the sacred domain of Apollo, whose favours the ancient Hellenes craved and whose wrath they feared.

'Nothing could surpass this, surely!'

'Unbelievable as it may seem to you, it does. The site and setting of the Sanctuary are quite beyond description.'

His tones were cool, dispassionate, as he went on to explain that the best times to visit the shrine were in the early morning, when the quality of light was less intense and the landscape softer, or at night when the moon was full. He did not add to this, but Marika could imagine what it must be like when everything was picked out in silver, with gleaming Mount Parnassus guarding the sacred precincts, and she said on impulse, speaking his name without embarrassment,

'Will you take me, Nickolas? – and tell me all about it?'

His glance flickered in faint surprise before he said,

'Perhaps – though you can learn everything in half an hour by going along and tacking yourself on to one of the guides.'

'Oh, no, I don't want to find out about it like that! I would rather go early in the morning, as you say, or late at night.' She hesitated before adding, in tones less confident, 'I would like to learn about it from you, when we're alone – without all those tourists, I mean.'

Some hint of emotion crossed his face before he spoke; her childish anxiety as she awaited his response seemed to touch him and his mouth relaxed.

'Very well, I will take you.'

'Soon?' she asked eagerly, regaining her confidence.

'Soon,' promised Nickolas gravely, and they walked in silence back to the car.

The sun fell quickly and it was almost dark when at last they entered Delphi, a straggling village perched on rocky terraces cut in the mountainside. Passing through the single street, they drove for a short distance before Nickolas turned into a driveway and brought the car to a halt before a low white building set amid flowers and trees.

Taking her suitcase from the car, he opened the door with a key and led the way upstairs. Marika followed, rather apprehensively, for there seemed to be no one else

27

in the house.

'This is your room.' Snapping on the light, he stood aside for her to enter. She expressed her appreciation with a little gasp. Everything was new, and modern, from the furniture and carpet to the pretty curtains fluttering from the window.

'It's lovely!' she exclaimed, going further into the room as Nickolas crossed over to the window and closed it.

'I had it re-furnished,' was all he said, though Marika later learned that it had been a sort of spare room, furnished with all the bits and pieces that no one else wanted. 'There's a wonderful view from here, but of course you cannot see it tonight – you will have noticed that darkness falls quickly here,' he added. 'The long evenings are probably one of the things you will miss, at least for a time.' He returned his attention to the view. 'Down below is the gorge of the Pleistus, and right across there the plain of Amphissa. Those lights you can see below are from the Bay of Itea in the Corinthian Gulf.' He paused. 'We are not overlooked – but perhaps you would prefer the curtains closed?'

'Yes, please.'

'That is your bathroom; I'm afraid it is rather small. I had it built over the garage so that you – or whoever came – would have their own.' He spoke in the now familiar quiet tones, curt and clipped. But Marika could detect a hint of anxiety as he added, 'I hope you will be happy here. If there is anything else you want, let me know. And now, perhaps you would like to tidy up after the journey, but be as quick as you can, for we must go in to Father. Come straight to me when you are ready; I shall be in the room to your right as you come down.'

With that he left her, and she tried not to think of the meeting with his father, for it seemed impossible that she could play her part convincingly. She marvelled that Nickolas remained so calm, so unperturbed. Musing on this attitude of his while she washed her face and brushed her hair, she found to her surprise that all her fears were subsiding. There was nothing to worry about; Nickolas would guide her quite safely through the coming ordeal.

Nevertheless, she could not truthfully admit she felt eager for the meeting and, after a glance in the mirror had satisfied her that she looked fairly presentable, she crossed the room and opened the window again. The air fanned her cheeks, invigorating, heady. The black outline of the mountains, the shadowy expanse of plain, and the twinkling lights from far below in the little bay, which from this distance appeared to be land-locked, gave her a sense of unreality, and with a sense of shock she realized all that had happened to her in a little over twenty-four hours.

She sighed, wondering just how far from home she was. The twins would be preparing to go out; her mother, too, would be going out, for there was a whist drive at the chapel hall every Thursday evening. And David . . . what would he be doing? He must know by now that she had gone. Perhaps he already regretted hurting her — perhaps he already missed her. She decided to write to him; after all, they had not quarrelled, so there seemed no reason why they should not correspond.

Feeling almost lighthearted, she closed the window and left her bedroom to go downstairs. Then, from somewhere at the far end of the landing, she heard a crash, followed by a man's voice uttering words she could not understand. But there seemed to be an urgency in them and, without stopping to think, Marika sped along the landing to the room from which she thought the sounds had come. Opening the door cautiously, she then entered the room.

The man on the bed had obviously been reaching for something from the table and had knocked the tray on to the floor. The jug and glass were broken, and a wet patch spread over the carpet. The man, however, was perfectly all right; he sat straight up in bed and stared at her.

'I'm sorry – I thought you needed help,' stammered Marika, bending down to pick up the broken glass and put it on the tray. She played for time, trembling already as, too late, she regretted her impulsive action in coming here. Without Nickolas's support she would be bound to blunder – disastrously.

'Who are you?' he demanded in excellent English, and in the same deep tones as those of his son, though he had a slight accent that Marika found rather attractive.

'I'm Marika.' She straightened up, aware of an odd light suddenly entering the man's eyes at the mention of her name. She stood looking down at him for a moment through wide, frightened eyes. 'I – I've come from England.'

'That's obvious. But what are you doing here? Marika, you say? Once had a friend who called his daughter Marika.' His penetrating gaze seared into her and for a while she could not speak. How like Nickolas! – with the same dark, forbidding countenance and piercing eyes. But his hair was wispy and grey, and the lines of his face were no longer firm. No evidence in his expression of the grave anxiety of which Nickolas had spoken, but his hands gave him away. White and frail, they clutched the bed cover, moving all the time as if providing a release for some kind of inward torture.

'Nickolas brought me,' she said at last. 'We've just arrived.'

'Nickolas?' he frowned. 'He's back? Why hasn't he been in to see me? He always comes right away. Where is he now?' And, without giving her time to answer that he added, 'He threatened to get me a nurse, but I'll not have one. Pitsa can look after me quite well!'

'I'm not a nurse. I'm his – his—' Marika broke off, panic-stricken. She had no idea of the way in which Nickolas proposed to explain his sudden engagement, but she knew he'd have some feasible explanation ready.

If she told Mr. Loukas who she was, she must be prepared for further questions, and these she could not answer. Her one impulse was to flee from the room, remembering Nickolas's warning that if she were to make one slip all would be lost. The old man now regarded her with some suspicion, which could only be expected, seeing that she just stood there, as if suddenly struck dumb.

'Yes,' he prompted at length. 'You're his . . . what?'

Marika swallowed convulsively, and began once more to stammer.

'Nickolas and I – that is, we—'

'There you are, my love. I wondered where you had got to.' Nickolas slipped an arm about her shoulders and she sagged with relief. 'So you have already introduced yourself?' and as she shook her head, 'Father, may I present my fiancée?'

The silence could be felt; tense, profound. The old man's lips moved soundlessly. He seemed all at once to be very frail and he leant back against the pillows in an attitude of exhaustion. Two large tears rolled down his cheeks and fell on to the sheet. The sight of a man in tears moved her deeply and she turned in the circle of Nickolas's arm, her eyes imploring him to comfort his father.

Nickolas removed his arm and, taking one of the old man's hands, he held it between his own.

'I'm sorry, Father. Has this been too much of a shock for you? Perhaps you would like to rest, and we will come back in a little while?' His voice was low and tender and there was an almost miraculous change in his expression as he looked down at the wasted face. 'Shall I fix your pillows for you?'

'I will rest – in a moment.' A certain strength entered again into his voice. 'Yes, I think I must.' He sighed deeply. 'Is this true, Nickolas? Are you and this – little one betrothed?'

'Quite true, Father. Marika and I are engaged to be

married.' Those calm tones had their effect. A subtle change came over the old man's face. 'Marika is to live with us from now on.' Nickolas paused before adding, with a smile, 'I rather think we can be sure of your blessing.'

'My blessing. . . .' His gaze became fixed on Marika; she met it unflinchingly. 'Give me your hand, little one,' he said, and Marika obeyed, feeling strangely drawn to this man who was so like Nickolas. 'My son has chosen well – he is a lucky man. But you, Marika, you are lucky, too. Remember that always. And now you can tell me, Nickolas, how this has come about? Why haven't I heard of Marika before?'

Marika listened, fascinated, as Nickolas in calm and even tones explained first who she was, and then went on to talk of her mother's request for help.

'I decided to go to England and see her. I think you would approve of that?'

'Indeed, yes. My dear friend's widow. I would not wish her to be in financial difficulties.'

'As you know, she has three daughters. Marika is the youngest. We met and—' He broke off, shrugging. 'Well, that was it!'

'Love at first sight, eh?' The old man leant further back into his pillows with a tranquil smile on his lips. He released Marika's hand and she put it to her cheek in a vague gesture of wonderment. Remembering David's teasing comments on her plainness, she could not help but be flattered by Mr. Loukas's assumption.

'Marika consented to become engaged to me,' Nickolas went on, ignoring his father's comment. 'I did not say anything to you. You see, at first, Mrs. Vaughan was not happy at the idea of Marika's coming away with me.'

A gasp of incredulity almost escaped Marika at this expert handling of the affair. The most amazing thing was that Nickolas had not yet told a lie.

'Naturally. She is a mere child; her mother would be anxious.'

'She was,' agreed Nickolas smoothly. 'Extremely anxious. However, you can imagine that I was unwilling to have my fiancée living so far away?'

'Of course.' The old man's tones were dry.

'So eventually Mrs. Vaughan was persuaded to allow Marika to come and live with us.'

'Most self-sacrificing of her,' he commented, turning to rest his eyes on Marika. 'It must have been a difficult choice for you, too, my child?'

A question, requiring an answer. The room became still; Marika's expression was guarded but speech failed her. She could hardly tell the truth, and she was not prepared to lie. Nickolas came to her aid, as she rather thought he would.

'Marika did not have much choice. I'm afraid I coerced her shamefully,' he admitted, and again Marika gave an inaudible gasp. Once more he had ready the most convincing reply. His father, completely taken in, emitted a low chuckle and cautioned her to beware of her fiancé's tyranny, though he did go on to say that he felt sure she would soon learn how to manage him without much difficulty at all.

Nickolas's face was expressionless, but noticing again the hardness of his eyes and the inflexible line of his jaw, Marika decided that anyone attempting to manage a man like that was asking for trouble in plenty.

They talked for a few minutes longer, Mr. Loukas asking Marika questions about her home and family, questions she answered without difficulty. She noted with extreme satisfaction that his demeanour had become one of complete tranquillity; his hands, so thin and frail, lay on the bed cover, relaxed and still. Whatever difficulties lay ahead, and Marika had an odd premonition that there would be many, she was glad she had come, happy to be doing something worthwhile by bringing peace to this man who had been so good to her family, and who had so little time to live.

He would have continued to ask questions, despite his obvious exhaustion, but Nickolas firmly brought the conversation to an end.

'Rest for a while, now,' he said, and his father obediently slid down into the bed. 'Are you quite comfortable?'

'Comfortable . . . and happy. You have made me very happy this day, Nickolas.' He looked up at his son, pausing before his next words. 'I have been very foolish, I think.'

'You have.' Nickolas fixed the bedclothes and straightened up. He and Marika were at the door when the old man spoke in Greek and Nickolas turned.

'Yes, Father, you're puzzled about something, you say?'

'You have not told me how long you've known Marika. I presume you did not become engaged on your first meeting?'

With a catch of her breath Marika saw, for the first time, doubt in the old man's eyes – doubt and even suspicion. Without hesitation Nickolas replied. He smiled, resting his hand on the door knob, in an attitude of complete unconcern.

'You will recall that I have made quite a number of – er – business trips lately. In fact, on several occasions you have complained about my being away so much.'

'You said you were buying two hotels, one in Patras and the other in Crete—' His face cleared and a sudden twinkle entered his eyes. 'Nickolas, I think you have been – what do you say, Marika? – a black horse?'

'Dark horse,' she corrected with a laugh.

'Dark horse, yes. But I will forgive you, my son, because you have brought this little one to make me happy.'

It was soon clear that Nickolas's gentleness didn't extend to Marika; once outside the room she became profoundly aware of his wrath, and on entering the sitting-room he rounded on her, demanding to know why

34

she had acted contrary to his instructions.

'Do you realize you almost ruined everything? Had I come along a moment later you certainly would have done so!'

'I heard a crash, and then what sounded like a call for help,' she explained apologetically. 'What else could I do but investigate?'

'You could have ignored it! Father is always knocking things over, and he invariably chides himself for his clumsiness.'

'Well, I wasn't aware of that!' Marika was stung into the retort, even at the risk of increasing his anger. 'You could hardly expect me to know what to do.'

Nickolas spoke very softly.

'I expected you to do as you were told. This is the third time that you have disobeyed my instructions. Let me warn you from the start, Marika, that when I say a thing I mean it. You'll find life much more pleasant if you remember that and act accordingly.' And without giving her the chance to reply to that, even had she wished to, he opened a jewel box which lay on the table and told her to choose one of the rings it contained. Marika then knew a moment of indecision. She had not even thought about a ring, and she hesitated, checked by the rather frightening conviction that, once she had placed his ring on her finger she would be bound forever to this dark and sinister Greek, that he would hold her, imprisoned, never to know freedom again.

What a stupid notion! Marika gave herself a little shake, recalling his arrogant disdain when she'd ventured to ask if he could force her into marriage. Nickolas no more wished to be bound to her than she did to him. No, some day the ring would be returned; she would be back in England with her family, and Nickolas would once again become the rather nebulous person from whom they received their cheque once a month.

He moved impatiently; Marika picked up one of the

rings and tried it on, glancing at him with considerably heightened colour as she did so. His eyes glinted strangely and she thought she detected an interest in her choice which seemed quite unnecessary under the circumstances. She returned the ring to the box and chose another.

'This one will do.' She fingered it awkwardly, feeling sad and thinking of David and of how she had vaguely expected one day to be wearing his ring.

'Are you sure? That is the one you prefer?'

'N-no . . . I like the solitaire, but it's too big.'

'We can soon have that put right. If you must wear a ring it might as well be one you'll enjoy wearing.' He held out his hand for the one she had on; she passed it to him, taking the diamond solitaire, surprised at his consideration, which seemed totally uncharacteristic. 'I go into Athens regularly, so will have it put right for you. In the meantime, perhaps you will try to manage with it. My father will expect you to be wearing a ring.'

'Yes, of course.' It struck Marika that Nickolas had intended giving her the ring before introducing her to his father, and she sighed with relief that the old man hadn't noticed its absence, for although it could easily have been explained away, she did not suppose Nickolas's temper would have undergone any improvement during the process.

He had ordered tea while she was upstairs, and it came now, brought in by an elderly woman dressed completely in black. She spoke to Nickolas in Greek; he said something in return, including Marika's name, and after she had put the tray on the table the woman smiled at Marika and said, in broken English,

'Welcome to Greece, Miss Marika.'

Marika coloured hotly at this form of address, murmuring her thanks in tones barely audible.

'Anna, the housekeeper,' Nickolas explained when she had gone. 'Been with my family for many years; she doesn't speak much English.' He began to pour the tea, telling Marika to draw up a chair and sit down. She sat stiffly, on the edge of the chair, facing him.

The elegant shuttered room, its furnishings and rugs distinctly oriental in character; the silver tea-set and exquisite eggshell china; Nickolas, remote and cold, his face harsh in the lamp light . . . all these combined to give her a sense of inadequacy. She felt gauche – and dismayed at the prospect of taking tea with Nickolas in what, she felt sure, would be an atmosphere of silence and constraint.

But, aware of her awkwardness, he spoke conversationally in tones less clipped than those with which she had become familiar. He told more about his family, giving her a rough outline of the routine with which she would be expected to conform.

Anna ran the house, with expert efficiency, although Hilary sometimes supervised. However, Marika learned that Hilary's main occupation was with the business; she helped Nickolas a good deal, and appeared to be an efficient and shrewd businesswoman. She sometimes worked with Nickolas in the office, an attractive building which Nickolas had had erected at the bottom of the garden. She sometimes took over the management of a hotel if the manager happened to be ill, or she could take the place of the receptionist if the need arose. In fact, she seemed to be invaluable to Nickolas, for obviously she could turn her hand to anything. Pitsa was a favourite with her cousin, and Marika suspected this was owing to her tractability and obedience. She did almost everything for her Uncle Stephanos and in addition helped her aged grandmother, with whom she took tea each afternoon.

Apart from commenting on her business acumen, Nickolas spoke little of Hilary, though he did mention that she never entered his father's room. How Hilary could continue to live here under those conditions Marika did not know, and fell to wondering if there might be something between her and Nickolas, after all. There seemed no other reason why she should wish to remain in the home to which Andreas had first brought her.

'Does she know that you intended bringing me back as your — your fiancée?' Marika asked the question tentatively, for it seemed an impertinence to question him at all.

'I haven't seen her since I decided to produce a fiancée,' he said. 'She is at present in Corfu, taking the place of the receptionist, who is ill.' His voice when he mentioned Hilary seemed always to contain a certain coolness, she thought. 'Like Father, she'll be surprised. Souphoula knows – she is my father's mother.' He went on to describe Souphoula who, though nearly ninety years of age, was too proud and independent to give up her home. Nickolas spoke of his grandmother with an underlying affection, but there was no doubt that she had a stiff, austere personality, and as Marika tried to form a mental picture of these people with whom she must live, it seemed that Stephanos and his niece were the only two whom she was going to like.

CHAPTER THREE

A FORTNIGHT later Marika was sitting by the bed, reading to Stephanos, when the sound of heavy breathing told her that he had fallen asleep. She lowered her book on to her lap, reflecting on the events of the past two weeks, and the ease with which she had slipped into the life here, adapting herself far more quickly than she would ever have thought possible. Perhaps it was because she'd found such a pleasant companion in Pitsa, or because Stephanos had taken her to his heart, extending to her the kind of affection she had missed since the death of her father. Or it could be owing to the fact that Nickolas did not trouble her overmuch with his company. He had spent a good deal of time in Athens, on two occasions staying overnight, but often he would start out very early in the morning and return in time for dinner. On those days when he remained at home his time was spent either in his office or with his father. It was also customary for him to spend an hour or so with his father each evening after dinner, and Marika naturally went with him.

As was to be expected, she made several minor slips, and although these passed unnoticed by Stephanos, they invariably brought her darkling glances from Nickolas. She made an almost irreparable blunder when one evening Stephanos decided to amuse her by relating some of the marriage customs of Greece. As he described the ceremonies performed over the preparation of the marriage bed Marika, so embarrassed as to be forgetful of everything save that her engagement was only a sham, exclaimed impulsively,

'How awful! Thank goodness I shall never have to go through all that!' And in the silence following her words she dared not look up to meet the amazement and

39

doubt that must surely have entered the old man's eyes.

Nickolas laughed.

'Marika knows those customs survive only among the peasants.'

'Knows? So soon . . . how can she?'

'She's a great reader, Father; surely you have already realized that?'

The old man's face cleared; he smiled faintly and changed the subject.

Marika sighed with relief, expecting to hear no more about her mistake, but she soon guessed that even Nickolas had experienced some alarm for, once downstairs, he shook her so thoroughly that she started to cry.

'Oh, Nickolas, don't! I'm sorry – it's with not being properly engaged.'

'That's your trouble!' he shot at her wrathfully. 'You're for ever conscious of pretence. Do you suppose you can go on for months *pretending* we're engaged! You and I *are* engaged – get that firmly fixed in your head and the rest will be easy!'

'But it's still acting a part,' she protested, 'and that's much more difficult than you seem to think.'

'Rubbish! The ability to act has always been a woman's greatest asset!' The cynicism of that was clear, but Marika refrained from making any comment which, she felt sure, would only increase his ill humour.

Yet the lesson did her good. Fear of Nickolas, coupled with her anxiety about his father's peace of mind, spurred her to a determined effort at living the part as Nickolas had advised. This she found easier than anticipated, and for a short spell she basked in her fiancé's approval before again incurring his displeasure.

'Try to show some slight measure of affection,' he snapped. 'Must you sit there as if expecting to be beaten any moment? Have I ever given you reason to be afraid of me?'

'No. . . .' she began, thinking of how he had shaken her

and then stood over her, his face like thunder. Mechanically she touched her arms where he had hurt them, leaving dark little bruises which she kept covered. 'No,' she repeated, because it was much more comfortable not to argue with him.

'Well then, let me see you be a little more natural.'

Stephanos stirred in his slumber, jerking her back to the present. Closing her book, she put it on the table, then softly left the room, closing the door noiselessly behind her.

Pitsa was in the sitting-room, her head bent over a sweater she was knitting for Marika, but she glanced up with a quick smile of welcome as Marika entered.

'Is Uncle Stephanos sleeping?' Pitsa held up the front of the sweater to view the length.

'Yes, but I expect he will waken shortly for his tea. Shall *I* get it?' Marika sat on a low stool, facing Pitsa, and wondering why those brilliant dark eyes shadowed now and then as if reflecting some secret unhappiness or disappointment. Pitsa had the same colouring as her cousin, but none of his arrogance. She was small and dainty, and seemed to occupy the whole of her time doing things for others. Her attitude towards Nickolas was one of deference amounting almost to humility; Marika felt she lacked spirit and wondered if her cousin had crushed any she might once have possessed.

'No; it's good of you to offer, but Uncle Stephanos likes me to prepare it, and take it up to him. He's a dear, but gets the oddest notions sometimes, and if I did not keep to the usual routine he might just get it into his head that he becomes a nuisance to me.' She spoke with a slight accent which lent an added charm to her rather husky voice; she also occasionally muddled her sentences, and this Marika found equally attractive. 'The colour, it suits you,' Pitsa went on, holding the knitting up against Marika. 'Nickolas might think it is too bright, but he will give your way to you, because he is in love.'

In love? How little she knew! Marika felt a hypocrite. Pitsa was so sweet and sincere that it seemed wicked to deceive her. Marika would have liked to confide in her, but instead she mentioned something that had puzzled her from the first.

'You did not seem surprised when Nickolas introduced me as his fiancée – at least, not as surprised as I expected you to be.'

Pitsa wound the knitting round her needles and stuck the ball of wool on the end.

'I was surprised – very much, because Nickolas has never been serious with anyone before.'

'But you didn't show it; you didn't ask him all the questions I would have asked had I been in your place.'

'Question Nickolas?' She sent Marika a glance of shocked reproof. 'I would never take such a liberty. Nickolas's affairs have nothing to do with me. No, I would not ask him intimate questions like that.'

'I cannot see that there would have been any harm in your being curious,' Marika said reasonably, then decided to drop the subject, lest Pitsa should expect *her* to explain. 'Have you never had a boy-friend, Pitsa?' she asked, thinking of David and wondering if he would reply to her letter.

Pitsa's face clouded and her eyes darkened with that hint of unhappiness that had puzzled Marika on several occasions. She appeared hesitant about replying.

'I did have one, but Nickolas made me give him up.'

'Why?' asked Marika, frowning, and again that long silence as Pitsa hesitated.

'He is – what do you say for it? – a rake. But he wouldn't be if we were married,' she added hastily. 'He has pillow friends, but all single men do in Greece. I think it unfair of Nickolas, because I daresay *he* has had many pillow friends, too.'

'P-pillow friends?'

'I do not know what you say for them in England –

42

perhaps your men do not have them, because I have heard they are so cold.'

Marika flushed at the casual way in which Pitsa spoke; she felt surprised, too, for Pitsa seemed all innocence.

'Nickolas has – pillow friends?' For one fleeting moment she allowed her imagination free rein. Nickolas, so grim and forbidding. Who could possibly want him for a pillow friend? She shuddered visibly and Pitsa hastened to reassure her.

'He had them – I should think – but he won't have them now. You will never need to have anxiety about Nickolas, so don't let it upset you, Marika. The Loukas men are traditionally faithful.' She smiled, her sadness gone, or hidden, and after putting the sweater away in a drawer, she went out to the kitchen to prepare her uncle's tea.

Marika reflected for a while on what Pitsa had told her, and remembering what Nickolas had said about her not being allowed to go far without a chaperone, she wondered how Pitsa had managed to meet the young man in the first place. But it didn't require much effort to imagine Nickolas's reaction on discovering what was going on. Pitsa must have had a most unpleasant time. Yet Marika had to agree that Nickolas was right in putting an end to the affair, for it would not be good for Pitsa to marry a man like that. She deserved someone far better. Marika thought once again about David and wondered, with a tightening of the muscles in her throat, if he had ... pillow friends. What did it matter if he had? What difference could it make to her now? And yet she knew that deep down inside, she still cherished the hope that they would one day be together.

Half an hour later Pitsa reappeared. Stephanos had almost finished his tea and had told Pitsa he could manage to remove the tray himself. Hesitating uncertainly for a moment, Pitsa then asked Marika if she would care to accompany her to Souphoula's for tea.

'I never like leaving you to take tea on your own,' she added. 'Perhaps when Nickolas is not so busy he will try and be at home more.'

'He does have tea with me quite often. Thank you for the invitation, Pitsa, but I'm afraid I have not made a hit with your grandmother.' Marika spoke with regret. 'I sometimes wonder if she dislikes the English.'

'It is her way; she is cold and stern, but she has not anything against your people. Here in Greece we very much like the English.' Pitsa smiled – as most people smiled at you in Greece, thought Marika.

She had been into the village several times with Pitsa; always there had been the curious stares, the questions shot at Pitsa, then the inevitable smile of warmth and welcome for Marika herself. Already she had a great admiration for the Greeks. Thinking of the disasters which had so often overtaken them, she marvelled that they could have remained so inherently cheerful. Nickolas seemed in many ways the exception, being taller, for one thing. Few men she had seen were as tall as he, and many were short and rather stocky. Nickolas also lacked the warmth, the responsiveness of the average Greek, but he lacked, too, that innate curiosity which proved so disconcerting to the average foreigner. On the one occasion when she had ventured out alone, Marika had not only been subjected to much questioning – in surprisingly good English – but had actually been touched and even prodded. It would seem almost as if they were trying to discover what she was made of!

Pitsa waited hopefully; Marika, deciding at length to go with her, went upstairs to tidy her hair.

Mrs. Loukas lived about a quarter of a mile along the road, in the direction of the village. She owned a small cottage at the end of a row. Like all the houses in the village, it stood perched on its rocky terrace, an atom in a world of endless space and towering crags. The sun, dropping swiftly, cast into a strange brilliance the massive

44

peaks of the Phaedriades, truly 'The Shining Ones'. From the sea a vague, elusive mist blew in to hover across the olive-laden plain of Amphissa, and overhead the eagles planed and swooped, their shadows dark against the glowing heights.

The cottage, unimposing and sparsely furnished, was gloomy and cold, yet suited to perfection its owner. She sat upright in a high-backed chair, her full black gown touching the floor. In her lined and sunken face only the eyes seemed alive, black, piercing, with all the frigid hauteur so pronounced in the eyes of her grandson.

Evincing no surprise at Marika's appearance, she spoke in English throughout the meal. When Marika would have gone to help Pitsa with the dishes the old woman called her back.

'Come here, child,' she ordered, and Marika moved hesitantly towards her. 'Why are you afraid of me?'

'I'm n-not,' lied Marika, startled by the woman's sudden interest.

Souphoula considered her for a long moment.

'Give me your hands.' Marika obeyed, though with reluctance. The swollen knuckle bones, shining through the parchment skin, nauseated her. 'Never think me ungrateful. I do in fact owe you a great debt. My grandson – he blackmailed you. Is that not what you would say in England?'

Marika smiled faintly at that.

'Nickolas had been giving us money for years. He merely threatened to stop the allowance unless I complied with his request. That can hardly be termed blackmail.'

The piercing eyes flickered strangely.

'You consider his action justifiable?' The knotted fingers lightly caressed the backs of Marika's hands. Marika stared down at her, so firm and erect, despite her great age. The black eyes still flickered.

'My father would have wished me to come,' said Marika quietly.

45

'I believe he would. My son often spoke of him, and with deep affection. He was a good man, I think.' Her gaze became intent. 'It must have been a wrench to leave your mother and sisters.'

Unwilling to mention the lack of affection in her family, Marika said nothing, but she felt the old woman would read her silence. If she did, she obviously had no desire to embarrass Marika, for she again mentioned her gratitude. And then, releasing Marika's hands, she listened for a moment to the sounds coming from the kitchen. Satisfied that her granddaughter was fully occupied with her task, Souphoula said, in tones devoid of emotion,

'You have probably already discovered that the Loukases are not a demonstrative family; nevertheless, our feelings go very deep. Nickolas is just as grateful to you as I am.'

A smile of amusement curved Marika's lips, and her dark eyes twinkled. Nickolas had an odd way of showing his gratitude! Marika's expression was not lost on Souphoula and the hint of a smile hovered on her own lips as she stated drily,

'So he's been bullying you already, though not seriously, I gather. He has a short temper, that one, which can be most unpleasant. Not a Loukas trait, must have got it from his mother. Don't let it disturb you, child. Nickolas becomes dangerous only when his anger is suppressed.'

The entrance of Pitsa precluded any continuation of the subject, but Marika's eyes remained on the old woman's face, examining it in a new light.

And she knew without any doubt that here was someone she could trust. The knowledge gave her confidence and a sense of security. Hadn't Nickolas said that, should his grandmother like her, she'd have found a staunch and sincere friend? Marika knew instinctively that there was more than gratitude in those black eyes; the knowledge brought a smile of satisfaction to her face, and she saw to her surprise an answering smile come swiftly to the older woman's lips.

Dinner, never a pleasant meal, took place that evening in an atmosphere of constraint.

Nickolas had heard that Pitsa had been seen talking to Adolphos, her former boy-friend, in the village. They had met by chance, Pitsa asserted, frightened by the expression on her cousin's face. He clearly believed her to be lying, and Marika thought so, too, for she recalled the occasion.

Pitsa had suggested they go to the museum, but when they were almost there she made the excuse that she'd some shopping to do. Marika thought nothing of that until, over half an hour later, Pitsa had arrived at the museum looking extremely agitated and guilty. Moreover, she had nothing in her hand but her purse. Although puzzled at the time, Marika had quickly forgotten the incident, for Pitsa did not, of course, confide in her.

Even Marika felt herself trembling as she looked across at Nickolas. He was concerned about protecting his cousin, but she felt his anger to be out of all proportion. How could any harm come to Pitsa simply by her holding a conversation with Adolphos down there in the busy village – in the middle of the day?

The meal over, they all went upstairs to sit for a while with Stephanos, but Pitsa soon went to bed. Marika would have loved to go to her, but as she usually remained until Nickolas himself left his father, any departure from the routine would have to be explained.

For some time after Pitsa left silence reigned in the room as each became absorbed in thought. The old man spoke first.

'Little one, I have decided while I am lying here. As you will one day marry my son I wish that you will begin to call me Father.'

Startled, Marika sought guidance from Nickolas. To

47

call Stephanos Father would surely be carrying the deception too far.

'Marika will certainly do as you wish,' said Nickolas calmly. 'Isn't that so, my love?'

'Yes – of course.' A flush rose and on seeing it the old man smiled.

'We embarrass you, I see. But you will not find it so difficult, my child, for already there is an affection between us; don't you agree?'

Yes, she agreed. She had been profoundly aware of it from the first, for she never felt happier than when sitting by his bed, talking, or reading to him from one of the books she had brought with her. Most of all, she enjoyed listening to his numerous tales of ancient Greece, of the gods and the mythology. He described places she'd read about in a way that made them live, in a way that filled her with a yearning to go out and explore their wonders for herself. From him she learned that the road they had come along from Levadia to Delphi was one of the most romantic roads in all Greece. Nickolas had pointed out the mighty barren slopes of Mount Parnassus, and told her the names of other heights, but little else. He did not mention that they passed the lonely crossroads where Oedipus had so tragically slain his own father, thus fulfilling the prophecy given by the Oracle. He had told her nothing of the ancient history and legend connected with the region, or even how Apollo came, first to the gulf of Corinth, in the form of a dolphin, and then to Delphi where, slaying the monster Python, he snatched the Sanctuary from Ghea, the earth goddess, and made himself god of Parnassus and conductor of the Oracle.

The old man, with all the Greek's intense love of his country, had expressed surprise that Nickolas had apparently taken so little interest in his fiancée. Marika, aware of her mistake in revealing the omission, had tried to explain that Nickolas had been extremely tired by the long journey, so could not be expected to feel in a talkative mood. While partly agreeing with her, Stephanos still appeared troubled by his son's lack of interest in her, especially when he discovered she had never been out of the village, had not, in fact, even been to the archaeological site.

'He's so busy, and often doesn't get in till late,' Marika had hastily excused her fiancé's conduct, for a frown had appeared on the old man's brow that gave her a feeling of guilt. 'I can go with Pitsa, or by myself, for that matter.' Strange, she thought, how it seemed of tremendous importance that Nickolas should accompany her on her first visit to the shrine. She recalled the moment when, standing beside him, enthralled by the infinite scene of towering crags and untamed heights, of olive groves and dark ravines, she had been filled with that sense of isolation and timelessness. The moment would live for ever in her memory, so indelibly had it been impressed upon her mind ... a moment she would have shared with no one else, not even David.

The desire to visit the ruins, surpassed only by those on the Acropolis in Athens, had at times been so strong that to resist it became a physical and mental strain.

Yet, for some reason which she could not possibly explain, she had to wait until Nickolas fulfilled his promise and took her there himself.

Unaware now, as she sat by the bed, of her wistful expression, Marika looked up in surprise when the old man mentioned it.

'You are not all contentment, my child, and that is because Nickolas has neglected you.' His eyes were anxious as he turned to his son. 'Marika tells me you have not once taken her out, Nickolas, and that is neither thoughtful nor kind. Remember the little one is a stranger among us; you must not leave her to her own resources like this.'

It had never occurred to Marika that the old man would fret over his son's lack of interest in her; much less did she expect him to mention it. But he had done so, and in a way which gave the impression she'd been complaining about her life's being dull. This, perhaps, would not have troubled Nickolas in the least; what did trouble him was his father's peace of mind had been disturbed. That, she knew, he would not have, and she trembled at the prospect of the admonishment to come.

'I'm sorry, my dear.' Nickolas reached across the bed and Marika extended her hand, putting it into his. The gentle tones, the gesture, both so typical of the lover, contrasted sharply with the look he gave her. 'There have been several problems demanding my attention recently, but I think I can now take some days off in order to show you around. You must let me know where you wish to go.'

The promise evidently satisfied his father, for he lay back on the pillows, contentment on his face.

'You must take her into Athens – isn't that where you wish to go first, my daughter?'

'I. . . .' Flushing at the way he addressed her, she fell silent with embarrassment. Her wide eyes travelled from Nickolas's impassive countenance to the tranquil face of the man on the bed, and she felt trapped. Although still glad she had come, she experienced a sense of deep foreboding which caused her to withdraw her hand and rub it hard, as if to erase the touch of the strong brown fingers that had so firmly clasped it. Arrogance glinting, Nickolas watched her action, but it escaped his father, who waited in placid silence for an answer to his question. 'If Nickolas will come with me to the site I shall be satisfied,' she murmured, though all her anticipation, her childish excitement at the prospect, had been quelled by the knowledge that Nickolas would accompany her only to please his father. Why this insistence that he should take her? she wondered again. What difference could it make whether she went with him, Pitsa or, as he had at first suggested, on her own, tagging along with a group, and a guide?

But that would mean crowds and movement. She'd seen the coaches unload their tourists by the hundred, heard the incessant chatter of French, Italians, Germans, Americans. . . . All had their guides; all appeared content to view the most superlative, most incredibly beautiful ancient site in Greece in an atmosphere of noise and confusion of tongues, of snapping cameras and intolerable heat. She would never see it for the first time under those conditions. No, she must go after the crowd had departed – and, whatever the reason, she must go with Nickolas.

The old man had dozed, and silence crept into the room. An opportunity to escape, for tonight, anyway, her fiancé's reprimand, she thought as, softly, she asked him if she might go to bed. He nodded, but as she opened the door Stephanos woke up.

'Are you going, child?' he asked. 'To bed?'

'Yes, if you don't mind. I feel tired.'

Stephanos then said curiously,

'Don't you two kiss each other goodnight?'

'Naturally, Father, when we have left you,' came the quick and calm response from Nickolas. 'We usually leave together, as you know, and therefore say our good-nights downstairs. I intended following Marika, had you not wakened. As it is—' He paused just long enough to warn her. 'Come here, darling. . . .'

Hot colour flooded her cheeks. She watched, fascinated, as he approached her from the other side of the bed; then he stopped, waiting. The real command lay in his glance; Marika, her heart pounding, walked slowly towards him.

His embrace began gently enough, and the touch of his lips was a mere caress. But, looking up into the dark and sinister face, which held all the pitiless arrogance of the sun god himself, Marika shuddered her revulsion.

An insult . . . and vengeance followed swiftly.

She could not move for a moment, when he released

her, but stared up at him, bruised and shaken, her lips quivering piteously. The memory of David's boyish kisses brought tears to her eyes. So gentle they were, and timid. On her cheek or on her head, rarely on her mouth.

As Nickolas moved away she surprised the expression on his father's face; with a gasp of horror she realized that, despite his illness, despite his growing affection for her, he had actually derived a sadistic pleasure from his son's treatment of her.

Barbarians — both of them! Without another word she fled along to her room and, slamming the door, turned the key in the lock.

Flinging back the curtains, she opened the window and stood looking out, over the sacred plain with its vast expanse of olive trees, to the distant twinkling lights of Itea. The breeze blew cold and cleansing on her lips, but her body still trembled with the new emotion that engulfed her. Something had happened ... something terrifying. No longer the desire to visit the shrine with Nickolas, to be alone with him in the moonlight — or at any other time, for that matter.

David's letter arrived a few days later. Nickolas, a curious expression on his face, was examining the handwriting as Marika came downstairs. He handed it to her, noticing the blush which had become familiar. His attitude towards her had changed slightly since that night when he had so brutally kissed her. The arrogance had diminished, and he adopted an air of mocking amusement whenever the blush appeared. Marika, fully conscious that he played with her, knew also that he enjoyed his game. Taking the letter, she caressed it almost lovingly; the only letter she'd received from England, for neither her mother nor her sisters had yet replied to any of hers.

With a sinking heart she saw that Pitsa had already had her breakfast and gone along to Souphoula's to do the tidying up. Nickolas had decided to have a few days' holiday and this was the first of them. Normally he had gone out before Marika came down, so she rarely had the ordeal of taking a meal alone with him. Putting the letter beside her plate, she poured the coffee. Nickolas, absorbed in his newspaper, murmured a perfunctory 'thank you' as she passed his coffee to him before helping herself to rolls and butter.

At length he lowered his paper.

'Aren't you going to read your letter?'

Wondering at his interest, she picked it up and slit the envelope, wishing he'd resume his reading. But he continued to watch her closely as she scanned the four large sheets, skipping much until she reached the end. And then, her face glowing, she read the letter through once more, carefully absorbing its welcome contents, not caring whether Nickolas watched her or not.

'May I ask who writes to give you so much pleasure?'

'From David,' she answered naïvely. 'He's my boy-friend.'

A momentary frown darkened his brow, then he laughed outright.

'This must be the first time any girl has told her fiancé that she's had a letter from her boy-friend!'

The laugh transformed his face. The firmness remained, without the arrogance, the amusement without the mockery. Something stirred within her; she felt wary, afraid, and bewildered all at once.

'We're not really engaged, though,' she pointed out, 'so it doesn't matter.'

Nickolas cocked an eyebrow.

'I told you, my dear, to remember, always, that we are. While my father lives you and I are inextricably bound to each other.'

While his father lived. ... Marika frowned. There seemed something morally wrong in waiting for someone to die so that she could be free to live her own life.

'Can't he ever get better?' she asked on a note of sadness.

'No.' Nickolas hesitated, and then asked if she would care to tell him about her boy-friend.

Knowing full well his reason for changing the subject, she talked at some length about David, and when she had finished Nickolas had learned all there was to learn about their relationship.

'Do you really believe this boy is serious about you?' he asked with some amusement.

'I did at first, and then I didn't,' she admitted. 'But his letter is full of apologies for what he said on the day I came away. I believed then that it was all over; he likes me again now because he says in his letter that he missed me when I'd gone, and now he's discovered he'd rather have me than all the girls at college.' Her eyes shone because David had never said anything like that before. Nickolas's tone sounded strangely gentle as he said,

'As you know, my father could live for two years. Is this David willing to wait that long?'

'He knows about your father. In any case, he has more than two years to do at college.'

'At the end of that time you will marry?' His voice sounded amused again and he waited, curiously, for her reply.

'He hasn't asked me to marry him, but – yes, I expect we shall marry some day.'

'You do not sound too sure,' he said and, taking up an ornate silver basket containing the bread rolls, held it out to her. Mechanically, she took a roll, but made no effort to eat it. 'Marriage is a thing over which you have to be very sure, my child, and you're so young—' He paused as if recalling some incident with regret. 'I'm afraid I hadn't realized just how young.' With a sigh which appeared totally out of character, he picked up his paper and once more became absorbed in it.

When, later, Anna came to clear away the dishes,

Marika said she would go upstairs and read to Stephanos as usual.

'We'll go into Athens tomorrow, and stay the night,' said Nickolas. 'I'm sure you would like to do some shopping. After that we shall be free to do our sightseeing.' For today, he went on, he'd potter about the garden, spend some time with his father, and also catch up on some letter writing. Marika could only stare. Never had he been so human, or spoken to her in those tones, and all at once she realized just how tired he looked.

'It was Father's idea,' she said apologetically. 'I suppose I must have given him some reason for thinking I felt myself neglected, but it wasn't intentional. I wouldn't expect you to give up your time for me.'

He made no immediate reply, for Anna had reappeared and begun loading the tray again.

'Father is right,' he said when Anna had gone. 'I have neglected you. While he might live for two years, it is most unlikely. It would be a pity if you returned to England having seen so little of Greece.'

He not only looked tired but sounded it, too, and Marika spoke on impulse, in the most natural, easy manner she had ever used to him.

'It doesn't matter, Nickolas; I can go some other time. You drive into Athens and back so often, and it's too much. I would rather you stayed around and took a good rest—' She broke off, biting her lip as Nickolas put in smoothly,

'I may have insisted on your acting as if we were really engaged, but I must also insist on your remembering where you are. In my country the women do not give the orders.'

Snubbed, Marika turned away, but before she reached the door Nickolas informed her that, there being a full moon, they would visit the ruins that evening. She turned, the colour leaving her face.

'I don't want to go, after all,' she told him in a low

55

voice. 'At least, not tonight. I can go with Pitsa. . . .'

A curious expression entered his eyes. He spoke rather gently.

'Come here.'

Marika shook her head.

'Your father is waiting.'

'Come here, Marika.' But he went to her, made a gesture to take her hands, then changed his mind. 'You have nothing to fear, I shall not hurt you.'

She brought her head up with a little start of surprise.

'I don't expect you will,' she returned, because that seemed the polite thing to say.

'I frightened you the other night—' For a brief space the familiar hard light glinted, and his voice was cruel. 'Never insult me again, Marika.'

'No. . . .' Very close he came, and very strong her desire to step back. But she checked it, having no wish to see again that terrible fury unleashed. 'I'm sorry – I didn't think we'd have to . . . kiss.'

'Twice you insulted me. No woman has ever before considered my touch unclean.'

So that was it – just hurt pride! It seemed not only to excuse his conduct, but also to bring her unqualified relief.

'I'm sorry,' she repeated, thinking of what Pitsa had said about pillow friends, and wondering if he had had lots of women. Some day one particular woman would be the last, and from then on he would follow the Loukas tradition . . . and remain forever faithful.

CHAPTER FOUR

THE moon floating in a stainless sky, the silvered rock face of the Phaedriades and the valley of the Pleistus beyond, the mystic hush enveloping the sacred precincts, all combined to give Marika a sense of timelessness, of eternality. To murmur, to break the silence even by the merest whisper, would seem like sacrilege.

Again she was poised in isolation, once more the pain of rapture caught her throat. Surely no place in all earth or heaven could surpass this!

She looked up at the man beside her, his profile harsh in the moonlight, his shoulders erect. The thin lips were taut; she remembered their cruelty. He turned as if compelled by her prolonged stare and she saw the deep lines about his mouth, the lowering brow, adding to the impression of intensity and power. A god himself! But not the god Apollo, not the sun god. Hades, perhaps, Hades who had dragged Persephone into the blackness of the Underworld . . . to be his bride.

The air, intoxicating and clear – even for Greece – took on a sudden chill; she shivered, and Nickolas, in tones of thinly-veiled authority, told her to fasten her coat.

Standing amid the ruins of the holy shrine, on the spot proclaimed by Zeus to be the Navel of the Earth, Marika found no difficulty in understanding why the ancient Greeks came to regard Delphi as the very centre of the world. For in the solemn grandeur of the landscape lay a sense of the ultimate, as if from the farthest extremities of the earth all roads must finally terminate in this sacred place.

She and Nickolas, on their way from the village, had trodden the path of the suppliants of long ago, past the

Kastalian Spring, gushing forth from the deep ravine of the Phaedriades, along the rough and rocky Sacred Way, once lined with magnificent statues in marble, bronze and gold, past the treasuries, in ancient times bulging with riches from every part of the known world. And they had come at last to the Temple of Apollo, to the spot where the priestess, sitting on the divine tripod, announced the Oracle to all who came to seek advice.

They had spoken very little – though Nickolas had explained to Marika the original layout of the Sanctuary – and as they stood there, in a setting of moon-pale heights, with all around them the breathless hush and haunting echoes of a distant past, neither seemed inclined to break the silence.

But at length Marika stirred restlessly, and Nickolas glanced down at her once more.

'Are you cold?' he asked softly. 'Shall we go back?'

'Not yet. . . .' Odd that, having become afraid of being alone with Nickolas, she now wished this night could go on for ever, into the mists of eternity. But there was a gentleness about him tonight that disturbed her profoundly, that caused her heart to race and her mind to fumble with some strange intangible yearning. She thought of David, and longed for a return to that uncomplicated relationship, to be free of this magnetism which Nickolas had begun to exert upon her.

After that first snub, he'd been almost eager to make up to her for it, and he'd been kind and attentive the whole day. They sat with his father after lunch; Nickolas put an arm about her shoulders as they left the room. Merely for effect, to satisfy the old man, yet his hands were gentle on her shoulders and his smile held warmth as, once outside the room, he thanked her for the attention she had given his father. He had then gone out to the garden; Marika followed later expecting him to be working, but he lay in a chair and seemed to be fast asleep. She stood looking down at him, a brooding expression in her eyes. For the first time she saw his face in repose, and felt a stirring of her senses, an obscure desire. . . .

He had opened his eyes; smiled at her confusion. Away from the cares and problems of his work he seemed a totally different person as, patting the chair beside him, he had said,

'Get yourself some tan. You look out of place with that pale skin.'

For the early part of the afternoon she had lain there, listening to the incessant chirping of the cicadas, and lulled almost to the point of sleep by the caressing warmth of the breeze. Nickolas had brought out iced drinks, then insisted on her returning indoors. She must acquire a tan gradually, in readiness for the real heat of the summer.

Aware that they no longer had the place to themselves, Marika looked round, surprised at the number of couples who had appeared. Some sat on the steps of the amphitheatre, as if awaiting the performance of one of the ancient Greek tragedies; others wandered aimlessly among the ruins, hand in hand, or arms entwined. Lovers gathering memories, in the world's most romantic setting.

Marika heard someone say knowledgeably,

'This is where the Pythia inhaled the vapours which sent her into a trance. She then re-told what Apollo had dictated to her.'

The spell had been broken; Marika sighed for its loss, then with a smile at Nickolas she said, prosaically,

'Do you really believe she could predict – or was it all a fraud?'

He opened his mouth to speak, then hesitated.

'I wonder what you wish me to say?' was the surprising rejoinder. 'I believe I must not shatter your illusions.'

Marika laughed.

'Father has already done that. He maintains it was all one great conspiracy – that the priests of Delphi had their spies everywhere. He says that when the Pythia went into

59

a trance her mutterings were incoherent, and that the priests interpreted them to suit their own ends.'

'Well, that may or may not be true,' said Nickolas. 'But great confidence in the Delphic Oracle must have existed, for the city flourished in wealth and fame for many centuries.'

'Oh, many of the predictions did prove to be true. Herodotus mentions them, but he also refers to some which were not.'

'Herodotus! Is that what you read? Where did you get it?' he wanted to know, staring down at her in surprise.

'From Souphoula; she has lots of books like that – in English.'

'Ah, yes.' His face cleared. 'My grandfather's collection.'

'I want to learn as much about Greece as I can before I go home,' she said, and silence fell between them. Marika broke it, saying she found it more satisfying and exciting to believe in the veracity of the Oracle.

'Most people do,' he agreed. 'The game of make-believe is often satisfying, especially to the young.'

'I hope I shall never grow too old for the game of make-believe,' she returned seriously, and a rather sardonic smile curved his lips.

'I do not think you will, Marika, but sometimes the game of make-believe can have very disappointing results. Remember that, my dear.'

She felt somehow that he referred to her relationship with David, and wished she hadn't told him about it, for he treated it so lightly. Her friendships were not his affair; certainly he had no right to deride them.

More people had come on to the site. The temple, or what remained of it, seemed almost crowded, and Nickolas suggested they go back home and come along another night.

They'd come often, she knew that instinctively, but still she wished to prolong this first visit.

'Can we stay . . . just a little while?' she pleaded, without much hope of being indulged. 'I'd like to go right up there, to the top of the theatre.'

'Very well.' He smiled at her quick glance of surprise. And, as they began to climb up the seats of the vast amphitheatre, 'You had better give me your hand, in case you slip.'

She put her hand in his, remembering how she and David always strolled along like this and, unconsciously her fingers curled in the most natural manner round those of Nickolas before, flushing hotly, she realized what she had done. Her instinct was to withdraw her hand altogether, but, with that savage reprisal so vivid and recent in her mind, she kept her fingers where they were. And after a little while, stealing a sidelong glance, she surprised a flicker of emotion on his face and at the same time felt the slight responsive pressure of his touch.

Reaching the top, they turned to gaze down at the road twisting and snaking round the spurs and ridges of the mountain. She thought of the journey from the airport, gasping as she realized it was a mere four weeks ago. It seemed ages since she had left England, since she had seen her mother and the twins, and David. . . .

Again that sense of timelessness, of massive calm and space. How was Nickolas affected by it all? Had he become so used to this earthly paradise that he took it for granted? Could he no longer be intoxicated by its grandeur?

Standing erect, head and shoulders above her, he gazed silently across the barren, fretted landscape, dominated by the great Parnassus – sombre, mysterious guardian of this hallowed spot.

Marika, strangely content, knew that Nickolas was intensely perceptive of all he saw; never would he become immune to the spell woven countless ages ago by his pagan ancestors; never remain unmoved by the over-whelming impact of the wild majestic scenery and eagle crags of Parnassus.

And what of this sense of timelessness, of being suspended between heaven and earth? Did he experience it, too? Perhaps she would never know. She could not imagine an occasion when she could ask him about it.

'Can we sit down?' she whispered, and he merely nodded.

The temple, seen from this height, seemed more imposing, more awe-inspiring than ever. And that was strange, she thought, because so little of the original structure remained.

With the sudden realization that Nickolas still held her hand, Marika felt the strength and warmth of his clasp. She became relaxed and completely at her ease.

'Long ago, before the dawn of time,' she murmured, softly, reverently, 'Zeus the king of heaven sent out two eagles from opposite ends of the earth. They met here. And so Zeus lowered a sacred stone, the Omphalos, to show that this was the centre of the world.' A little silence followed her words; she sensed a new, amused indulgence in her fiancé and added on a sudden, childish impulse, 'Tell me about Apollo, Nickolas.'

'You sound extremely well-informed,' he returned drily. 'Perhaps you should tell me the story.'

Quite true, she was well-informed. What with Mr. Loukas and Pitsa, Souphoula and her books, it was impossible not to become absorbed in the history and mythology of this, the most famed of all the ancient Greek oracular sanctuaries. But she wished to hear the story from Nickolas, and she told him so. He hesitated and then Marika felt she could almost hear him say, 'This is your evening so, for once, I shall indulge your every whim'.

His voice, now lacking the familiar clipped, sharp edge, seemed gradually to take on a gentleness which added to her sense of quiet and ease. So well did he relate the story, so vivid did he make the events, that Marika forgot for a while her surroundings, the mountains and the moon, the people gathered below in the temple, as she followed Leto in her unhappy wanderings, searching for a haven in which to bring forth her immortal children, Artemis and Apollo.

Seduced by Zeus, and therefore hated by Hera, his wife, Leto fled from one island to another, but with Hera's wrath so greatly feared, she found herself repeatedly turned away. To add to her sufferings, Leto was harassed by the Python, whom Hera had sent to pursue her. At last Zeus, in his pity, sent the sea god, Poseidon, to conduct Leto to the island of Delos, where her twins were born.

Everything shone with Apollo's brilliance, which he shed all over the island. So arrived the god of purity, whose first act was to slay the Python, leaving it to rot on the southern slope of Mount Parnassus.

'That was the Greek manifestation of the power of light over darkness,' Marika interrupted impulsively. 'I think it's lovely!'

Being the son of Zeus, Apollo knew the will of his father – 'I will tell the people the right advice of Zeus' he promised, and established the Oracle at Delphi.

So rich did the city become that there were 'forests of statues', and even when three thousand were stolen the city was by no means depleted.

By the time Nickolas had finished his story Marika had again returned to her surroundings, her concentrated gaze fixed on the temple below. Apollo's most sacred domain!

'Nickolas, wouldn't it be wonderful to turn back the clock, just for a few minutes, to see what it was all like!'

He smiled faintly and said,

'Would you consult the Oracle?'

'Yes . . . I suppose I would,' she returned with a laugh. 'But what could I ask it?'

'About your future, of course.' His smile deepened as he played the game with her. 'Towards the end, when the

Oracle began to decline, people asked all sorts of frivolous questions as, for instance, "Whom shall I marry?"'

Whom shall I marry? Did she want to marry David? Yes, that was what she wanted, and yet. . . .

Silence came between them; a chill entered the air and Marika shivered, genuinely cold this time. Releasing her hand, Nickolas stood up, saying, with all his former curtness,

'We must go, otherwise it will be too late for a few minutes with Father. I promised him we would go in when we returned.'

'Pitsa, tell me about Andreas.' Marika stood at her bedroom window looking down at Nickolas and Hilary, standing together by the car. Nickolas held a duster, and every now and then he would stop talking and give the car a rub, though apparently without either energy or interest.

To Marika's bitter disappointment Nickolas had been forced to postpone their visit to Athens. The manager of his hotel in Corfu had been taken ill and Nickolas himself had gone over to take charge until his return. Nickolas was away a fortnight, and when he came back Hilary was with him. She stood beside him now; elegant even in shorts and a sun top. Marika, remembering that Nickolas had said her sisters were like Hilary, noticed her fair beauty and that poise and confidence which seemed always to be so attractive to men.

He stood smiling at Hilary and, with a little catch of her breath, Marika knew that his eyes held affection.

It was a week since Nickolas had brought her home, and during that time they had been so friendly, so companionable, that it seemed impossible to believe there was nothing between them. Odd, thought Marika, that Nickolas should be friendly with her, knowing how bitterly his father hated her.

What Nickolas had told Hilary about his engagement Marika did not know. After a rather intense scrutiny Hilary had adopted an attitude of indifference towards her, treating her at times almost as if she were an intruder.

Waiting for Pitsa's reply, Marika sensed the other girl's reluctance to speak, and turned inquiringly.

'Hilary's husband?' began Pitsa, looking uncomfortable. She had come up to bring her uncle's tea, and Marika had called her in to look at some bright woollen bags she had bought in Arachova, for her sisters' birthday. 'He was killed in an accident.'

'Yes, I know. Was he like Nickolas?' She knew Pitsa would not care to talk about Nickolas's brother, yet Marika could not contain her curiosity.

'He was ... kinder than Nickolas,' came the hesitant reply. 'I think he was too soft, too — what do you say? — lenient, with Hilary. In Greece always it is the man who is the— Oh, dear,' she smiled rather wanly at Marika. 'I do not speak your language very well, I think. In Greece the man must always be the — big one?'

'The master?' suggested Marika, turning once more to gaze down into the garden.

'That is it. But Hilary would not have that at all—' Pitsa broke off, a faint flush rising in her pallid cheeks; obviously she felt she had already said too much.

Still Marika wished to pursue the matter, though she had no idea of the reason. She explained to Pitsa that she was in possession of certain information regarding the Loukas family, telling her about Elaine, who had taught in Athens and had been friendly with the Pantelides family, who had since moved from Delphi. After learning this Pitsa seemed more willing to talk about Andreas who, though resembling his brother in looks and build, completely lacked his strength of character. Pitsa's words were carefully chosen, but, owing to her inability at times to find the appropriate method of explaining, she

65

revealed much more than was her intention.

Andreas had clearly been infatuated with Hilary, had even married her against the advice of his family. Her extravagance, her affairs with other men and her growing contempt for her husband had at last driven him to a state bordering on hysteria. After a particularly violent quarrel he had rushed out, got into the car, and driven like a madman on an icy, treacherous mountain road.

There was no doubt that Hilary, though indirectly, was responsible for her husband's death, just as Mr. Loukas had maintained. Yet Nickolas could adopt this friendly – no, more than friendly – attitude towards her! Had it been any other man Marika could perhaps have understood. But such apparent forgiveness seemed so contrary to Nickolas's character, in fact, Marika would have been far less surprised to learn that he had deliberately gone out of his way to punish Hilary for her treatment of his brother.

The pupils of Marika's eyes became intense and dark as she watched Hilary laughingly take the duster from Nickolas and rub away at some mark she had apparently discovered. Nickolas stood, smiling and watching. . . .

Marika, twisting the ring on her finger, reflected for a moment on Nickolas's reaction if she herself had snatched away the duster from his hand like that.

'They are very friendly,' said Marika, though she hadn't really meant to speak her thoughts aloud.

'Hilary and Nickolas?' Pitsa joined Marika at the window. 'Yes, they are,' she reluctantly admitted. 'I am sorry. . . .'

Marika frowned in puzzlement.

'What for?'

'It hurts you, I think?'

'Of course—' She had begun to say 'of course not', then pulled herself up just in time. How difficult it was at times to remember what was expected of her. 'Yes, naturally I do not like it,' she added, hoping she looked suitably upset.

'You are jealous?'

Unable to tell a barefaced untruth like that, Marika searched quickly for some convincing retort.

'No, just annoyed.'

'Annoyed . . .?' Pitsa considered this. 'I do not understand the English sometimes. I would be very jealous if my man paid so much attention to another girl.'

Nickolas's attention towards Hilary was even more pronounced than usual at dinner that evening. With a shock Marika discovered just how charming he could be, how gentle and considerate.

They had a guest, Kostos Matsoukis, a handsome Greek who, despite his youth, had recently been installed by Nickolas as manager of one of the hotels in Athens. He was twenty-four, and of a quiet, serious disposition.

He talked a good deal to Pitsa and Marika, yet his attention often strayed to Hilary. Marika had the strange conviction that he disliked her intensely; she also felt that a peculiar undercurrent ran beneath the lighthearted banter that passed now and then between Nickolas and his young employee.

Kostos left early, and Nickolas went to the door with him, telling Marika to go up to Stephanos. But, noticing that Pitsa had already gone to bed, Marika went to her, for Pitsa had not been happy during the meal, and had slipped away without a word to anyone.

She looked paler than ever, sitting there on the bed, staring before her unseeingly, a hand to her mouth, as if to still the trembling of her lips.

'Pitsa—' Marika sat down beside her, slipping an arm about her shoulders. 'What is it? I can't bear to see you like this – is it Adolphos?'

Pitsa nodded dumbly.

'He's gone away, to England.'

'To England?' Marika blinked at her. 'Whatever for?'

'His friend went last year, and found some work in

London. Now he has asked Adolphos to join him – and – and he's gone – without seeing me to say good-bye!' To Marika's dismay, Pitsa burst into tears.

'Don't, Pitsa, don't cry.' Marika's arm tightened. 'How do you know this?'

'We used to leave each other notes at the shop where I buy my wool. I had a note just before dinner. Katerina brought it up for me.' She was looking for a handkerchief; Marika gave her one, watching her in silence as she dried her tears. How risky to exchange notes like that! She trembled to think what would have happened had Nickolas discovered what was going on.

'Perhaps, in the end, it will all be for the best,' Marika said gently. 'I know how you must be feeling just now, Pitsa, dear, but I cannot help thinking that Nickolas is a very good judge of character. I'm sure he knows what is best for you.'

Pitsa looked round at her reproachfully.

'You chose your own husband, yet you think I should have the one Nickolas chooses. That is not at all fair, Marika.'

There seemed no answer to that. Marika felt helpless; she also felt extremely anxious. Nickolas would want to know the reason for this delay.

'The ways of your country are different,' she pointed out, rather lamely, whereupon Pitsa informed her that the odd customs she had read about existed only in the poorer, more backward villages.

'It is no longer usual for a girl in my position to be so carefully watched, so restricted!' But after that little outburst Pitsa appeared once more to become resigned, though she added, tragically, 'I shall never marry, now – never!'

When Marika reached Mr. Loukas's room the door stood ajar, and she could not help overhearing part of the conversation.

'I should like to see her married to Kostos,' Nickolas

was saying. 'Though she still frets over that rake, Adolphos.'

So that was why he'd invited Kostos to dinner! Marika suspected that, from now on, they would be seeing him quite often.

Stephanos began to reply in Greek, then broke off as Marika entered, smiling a welcome.

'There you are, little one. Sit down, my child.' A very quiet, gentle manner had come over him during the past week ... and a subtle change that brought a lump to Marika's throat.

Relieved that neither appeared to notice her lateness, she sat down by the bed, folding her hands in her lap. A book lay on the table; she read the Greek title, 'Oedipus Tyrannus' and smiled faintly. Stephanos, watching her, smiled, too, and asked how her Greek was progressing.

'She read *Oedipus* in her own language,' he told Nickolas, 'but when I explained what she was missing, she plunges right in and tackles Greek!'

Marika flushed, then laughed at her fiancé's surprise.

'I've learnt the alphabet, and about a dozen words—' She spread her hands. 'It is much easier to speak it than read it.' And that wasn't so easy, either, she reflected, thinking of her daily struggles with Pitsa.

'Keep on, though,' advised Stephanos. 'Do some every day, no matter how little, for this is your country from now on, and you will need to know the language thoroughly.'

She met her fiancé's gaze across the bed, receiving the message.

'Yes, Father,' she returned obediently. 'I shall continue to work very hard on it.'

Nickolas's approval was conveyed by the merest flicker of his eyes, yet Marika felt a warmth envelop her, and she gave a soft sigh of contentment. But, once again, she did not long bask under his favour. It had never occurred to her, when she had told Pitsa she felt annoyed at her fiancé's attention towards Hilary, that her friend would become so troubled as to mention it to Souphoula.

And Souphoula had later mentioned it to Nickolas. So when Marika met him coming in the following day, she found herself subjected to an icy and arrogant stare before he snapped,

'Come in here; I want to speak to you!'

She followed, slowly, her brow creased in perplexity.

'Is anything wrong?' she ventured nervously, trying to think of some slip she had made with Stephanos.

He observed her with the same chill hauteur for a while without speaking. Faintly, from the regions of the kitchen, came the strains of Greek music being played on the radio. Even that sounded ominous.

'Since when have you considered yourself in a position to express annoyance at my actions?' he inquired, and her frown of puzzlement deepened.

'I haven't — I don't know what you mean, Nickolas.'

'You told Pitsa that my interest in my sister-in-law annoyed you!'

The swift colour flooded Marika's cheeks.

'Pitsa told you?'

'She told Souphoula. Pitsa seemed most concerned, you upset her!'

'I didn't mean to,' she said unhappily. 'You see, Pitsa asked me if I were jealous, and as I couldn't truthfully say yes—' She stopped, aware that the footsteps she heard approaching were Hilary's.

'I have told you before to remember where you are,' Nickolas returned, his voice dangerously quiet now. 'Even if we were to be married you would not question my right to act as I please.'

The footsteps came closer.

'I will explain later,' began Marika, and was immediately interrupted.

'Don't trouble to explain, just keep out of my affairs,' he cautioned, and left the room as Hilary came in.

Hilary glanced from Marika to the door, and back again, her violet eyes flickering oddly. Sitting down, Marika took a newspaper from the couch beside her, trying to compose herself. From the first she had been overwhelmed by this woman's confidence, by her cold superiority. After a while she found herself scanning the headlines, seeing if she could spell out any of the words, now that she knew the alphabet. Hilary's voice, faintly sneering, cut short her efforts.

'You're not trying to convince me you are reading that?' she asked, and Marika said nothing. Life had been so pleasant before Hilary came, despite Nickolas's rather frequent scoldings, and Marika often wished that Hilary would go back to her job in Athens, or to Rhodes – or wherever else she might be needed. 'What's the matter with Nick?' Hilary went on, changing the subject. 'He seems to be in a foul mood. Have you vexed him?'

Marika nodded as she folded the paper carefully and put it back on the couch.

'Yes. He was angry about something I said.'

Hilary sat down, crossing one elegant leg over the other. Marika looked past her to the ikon fixed to the wall above an exquisitely inlaid sideboard, on one end of which stood a beautiful alabaster figure, replica of the 'Hermes of Praxiteles'.

'And now you've seen his temper, aren't you glad you're not going to marry him?'

Marika's lashes came down, veiling her expression. Why, she wondered, had that remark brought such a painful tightness to her throat?

'You know about our engagement's being a sham?'

'Nick and I are very great friends. I have always been in his confidence.'

Yes, their relationship was such that she must be in his confidence. For a moment Marika thought it was no wonder Mr. Loukas had reached the conclusion that there was something between them. But then she remembered that, as Hilary had not been allowed to enter his room since her husband's death, he could never have seen her and Nickolas together. And no one in the house would have upset the old man by telling him.

Hilary again changed the subject, asking Marika how she liked living in Greece.

'It's wonderful!' Marika returned enthusiastically. 'I love being here. And I think the people are wonderful, too!'

'The people?' Again that thinly-veiled sneer. 'I find the women dull, and so drab, especially in the villages. Pitsa, for instance, totally without character; and Souphoula— well, it's time she—' Hilary stopped, amused, at Marika's darkening brow.

'Pitsa is my friend,' she informed her quietly. 'As for Grandmother, I have a great affection for her, too. I am proud to know that she likes me.' Then she added deliberately, 'I hope she lives for a very long time.'

'She probably will,' said Hilary, shrugging. 'She has great stamina. How is the old boy upstairs, by the way?'

Odd, reflected Marika, that Nickolas did not keep Hilary informed about his father's condition.

'He is not very well, I'm afraid.'

'Of course he's not very well – hasn't been for years.'

What she really meant, then, was had his condition deteriorated? Could it be that she and Nickolas would marry as soon as Stephanos died? Somehow, Marika could not shake off the conviction that such conduct would be quite contrary to Nickolas's character.

'Sometimes,' said Marika evasively, 'he is much better than others.' Unconsciously, she gave a little sigh and her dark eyes were sad.

'Nickolas says he has taken a great liking to you.'

'I think he has.' A faint smile touched her lips. 'We have taken a liking to each other. Mr. Loukas was such

72

a good friend to my father – and to all of us.'

'So I believe, but they never saw each other for years.'

'They never saw each other at all after that first holiday. Father never had the money to come back, and I suppose Stephanos was always too busy to come and see us.'

'Seems odd that a friendship could survive under such circumstances.'

'You don't have to be with people to be their friends. You can be far, far away, yet be with them in thought.' Marika hadn't meant to think of David until she saw that flash in Hilary's eyes, that flash of curiosity.

'You have someone at home?' The voice was a purr, not the purr of a kitten, but that of a tiger, soft and menacing.

'I have a boy-friend,' she admitted. 'David.'

'So you are just as eager as I for—' She left the rest unsaid, amused by the spark of reproach that kindled Marika's eyes.

'I am in no hurry to go home,' and, excusing herself, Marika left the room, and the house, to make her way through the fresh, pure air to a little cottage clinging precariously to the side of the mountain.

CHAPTER FIVE

'SOUPHOULA, why are all Greek taxi drivers called Yanni?' Marika sat on the cool, clean floor beside the bookcase, examining its contents, trying to decide which book she would borrow next.

'They're not.' Souphoula, erect on a high-backed chair, her hands folded, looked down at Marika in some surprise. 'What gave you that idea?'

'The other day I went into Arachova to buy something for the twins' birthday. I wanted to go by bus, but Nickolas said to get a taxi. There was a whole row of them – they had brought parties of tourists up from Itea – and I asked one man if he would take me while his party were visiting the site. He couldn't, but told me to ask his friend, Yanni, further along the row. He hadn't time, either, and shouted to another driver. His name was Yanni—' She turned, a book in her hand, a look of puzzlement on her face. 'I was taken at last – by the fourth Yanni!'

The old woman smiled perceptively.

'Tourists expect every Greek male to be called Yanni, because it is a very common name here, so we always give the tourists what they want.'

'I think that is silly,' retorted Marika with disgust.

'It's an easy name to remember, and the tourists usually call the drivers by their Christian names immediately the bargaining is over. Did you bargain?' she asked, with a faint smile.

'Yes, and he knocked me ten drachmae off,' returned Marika proudly. 'And then we made harmony,' she added, using a familiar Greek expression.

'Made harmony, did you?' Souphoula's tones were dry. 'I hope you sat in the back of the taxi, my child.'

Getting up from the floor, a placid expression on her face, Marika sat on the stiff settee, taking care not to rest her head on the brilliant white cover.

'Yes, I did. But the Greek people do not mean anything wrong when they touch you, Souphoula, because the women do it, too.' Her eyes were serious, but she flushed a little at the old woman's obvious scepticism. 'Everybody pats you, and I'm sure they do it because they like you.' Thinking of the beautiful sculpture, Marika felt the tactility was bound to be inherent in a people who had produced such magnificent works of art. 'I do not mind in the least if they touch me.'

'Then it's a good thing you're not really engaged to Nick,' was the dry comment from Souphoula, 'otherwise you'd find yourself in trouble. I doubt very much whether he will ever marry, but if he does he'll make a very jealous, possessive husband, I'm afraid.'

Suddenly restless, Marika rose and moved to the window, drawing apart the heavy curtains which shut out the sunlight. It was July, and everything shimmered under a heat haze. The barren lofty massif, the vast unbroken sea of olives, the distant Bay of Itea. How remote the tiny Cheshire village, the soft and undulating land of home!

How long before she returned? Did she want to return? At times she longed for David, yet fretted at the inevitability of the death that would release her. Already she loved this country and its people, yet England somehow called.

And what of Nickolás? Often he repelled her; just as often he drew her. She half turned, to stare unseeingly at the dresser with its odd assortment of bric-à-brac, sponges and shells, tiny primitive votive offerings and ikons.

Her conflicting emotions held her, while Souphoula, straight, immobile, looked on, her sunken face expressionless but her black eyes watchful, mysterious, allseeing.

'I shall have to go.' Marika's thin face took on a sudden bleakness. 'I promised Father I would read to him before tea.' Yet she seemed reluctant to leave and the old woman said quietly,

'Sit down and tell me all about it.'

Closing the curtains again, Marika turned.

'About . . . what?'

'You didn't come here to ask me about the taxi drivers, or even to borrow a book. Is it Hilary?'

'I – I don't know what you mean.'

'You've been a different child since she appeared. She enjoys hurting people. What has she done to you?' The hooded eyes, dark and compelling, searched Marika's very soul. 'You came here to open your heart; do it, child, and let us sort things out!'

'I don't know why I came,' admitted Marika after a long, deliberating silence. 'I only know that here I find . . . peace.' A strange place to find peace, she thought, looking round, in the rather dismal half-light. The round table in the corner, the austere high-backed chairs in a row along the wall. A streak of sunlight, escaping through a chink in the curtains, only added to the impression of chill.

'Come to me, my child.' Souphoula held out her hand; Marika took it eagerly, recalling for a moment how its bony whiteness had at first disgusted her. A stool lay close by and, reaching for it, Marika sat down, her head against the billowing folds of Souphoula's long black skirt.

'I am so confused,' she murmured, relieved to be able to speak at last. 'Life seems to have become so very complicated.' And yet why? Nothing had changed. She would remain here until she was no longer required, and then she would go home. That had been the original arrangement, and that arrangement still stood.

'My grandson . . . what are your feelings for him, Marika?' The soft and gentle words brought no start of surprise from Marika. Pressing her head closer into the

76

folds of the old woman's dress, she admitted that she did not know, that at times he frightened her, and yet she knew instinctively that he would always exert some strange influence over her, that she would never be able to forget him. And then she leant away, looking up at Souphoula, her eyes darker than ever.

'Is he in love with Hilary?' she asked, and saw the old eyes narrow.

'Does he appear to be?'

'That is difficult to answer,' she confessed. 'Nickolas seems to like her very much.'

'So you're jealous of Hilary.' Souphoula's voice took on a harsh note. 'She will enjoy that, my child. You must endeavour to hide it.'

'Oh, no! How could I be jealous? I'm not – not—'

'Yes,' prompted the old woman softly. 'You are not in love with my grandson?' Silence reigned for a moment, Marika's gaze fixed on the ray of sunlight, picking out a threadbare patch of carpet. 'I think, my child,' the soft voice continued, 'that Nickolas should not have brought you.'

'I would not have it otherwise, Souphoula. My father would have wished me to come, to relieve Stephanos's mind.'

'I should not worry too much about Hilary,' said the old woman after a while. 'Nickolas was extremely fond of his brother, despite his many weaknesses. And,' she added with almost sinister deliberation, 'the Loukases are not a forgiving family.' The thin gnarled hand softly stroked Marika's head. Whatever happened, thought Marika, however difficult life were to become, always she would find comfort here, always have someone on whose shoulders she could lay her burden.

'I feel better now,' she smiled, standing up and taking her book from the couch. 'I must go; Stephanos will wonder what has happened to me.'

Two days later Nickolas announced his willingness to take Marika into Athens for a short visit. Marika suspected that either his father or Souphoula had pressed him to do this, but the knowledge did not detract from her pleasure. Her father had never tired of talking about the city, and she herself had read about its wonders, especially since coming to Greece.

The idea of being alone with Nickolas, although disturbing, was yet exciting, too. She remembered how, away from the cares of his work, he had been a different person.

Hilary, openly annoyed, suggested accompanying them, and Marika waited breathlessly for his reply.

'We do not require a chaperone,' he said curtly. 'Besides, there is work for you to do.'

His attitude puzzled Marika. Whatever his feelings for Hilary, he seemed determined to make her work.

They set out just after lunch, in almost unbearable heat, the sun blazing down from an incredibly blue sky. Nickolas, relaxed, and apparently in the mood to enjoy his holiday, stopped several times so that Marika could enjoy the view. He pointed out the lonely Triple Way, where Oedipus killed his father, and made a longer stop than previously at Levadia where they had refreshments at a little café on the banks of a stream. They saw the two streams, Mnemosyne and Lethe – Memory and Forgetfulness, and the cavern where dwelt the Oracle of Trophonius, once almost as famous as that of Delphi itself. Nickolas pointed out Mount Helikon, sacred to Apollo and haunt of the Muses.

They drove on through desolate mountain fastnesses, crossed the Plain of Thebes, descending all the time until, by early evening, Marika caught her first breathtaking view of the Parthenon, outlined against the violet-shaded backcloth of Mount Hymettus.

'Oh,' she breathed ecstatically, 'I never thought I'd ever really see it!'

Nickolas glanced at her for a brief moment, a smile

softening his lips.

'I have been neglectful,' he admitted, rather gently. 'We must see if we can't make up for it during the next few days.'

Immediately on arrival at the hotel in Syntagma Square, they went up to the suite of rooms which Nickolas had set aside for his own use.

Catching her breath at the luxury of the 'flat', Marika almost forgot Nickolas's presence as she moved about, glancing in at every room. And then she turned, guiltily, to see for the first time an odd smile of amused indulgence on her fiancé's lips.

'I shouldn't have done that,' she apologized. 'But it's so beautiful – I've never ever been in a place like this before.'

'You will sleep here,' he said, taking her suitcase into the bedroom. 'I'll find an empty guest room.' On the bed was a large box, and although Marika could not read what was printed on the lid, she knew what it contained, for with a sudden flash of memory she saw herself carrying a similar box on to the airport at Gatwick. 'I have had a few dresses sent along – I think they're the correct size,' he added, glancing at her figure. 'You're about the same as Pitsa. Pick out what you like and we'll send the rest back.'

'Thank you.' She smiled gratefully. 'You're very kind to me, Nickolas.'

'I wonder if I've been kind?' He seemed to dwell on that for a while, and then, rather more briskly, 'We'll dine here, in the hotel, then I am going to show you the Acropolis by night; the lighting effects are so spectacular that you will remember your first impression for a very long time.' And with that he left her, saying he would return in about an hour.

Marika examined the dresses, picked one out, then had a shower. While revelling in the luxury, she could not help feeling that her sisters would be much more at home

79

in this setting as, standing before the mirror, she was again reminded of David's teasing remarks about her plainness.

If her mouth were larger, and her nose not turned up *quite* so much. . . . Screwing up the ends of her hair, she tried to imagine it short. Perhaps she could have it cut some time, and styled. . . .

The dress she had chosen was of white embroidered cotton, sleeveless, with a mandarin collar – and very short. The girls at Delphi did not wear such daring clothes, but she had seen plenty of short skirts after entering Athens. With a shrug she fastened the zip. If Nickolas did not approve he would soon tell her to change.

And he did regard the length rather critically. Having merely ordered by telephone, he had not seen any of the dresses until now.

'Are they all that length?' he wanted to know, frowning.

'No,' Marika gave a little gesture of resignation. 'Shall I change?'

Nickolas opened his mouth to say yes, then the forlorn note in her voice penetrated. How little she had had, he thought, remembering those brilliant sisters of hers.

'I think that one will do – though you look like my daughter,' he added with a grimace.

'Oh, no!' she exclaimed quickly. 'You look very young tonight, and very smart.'

'Thank you.' His dry tone made her blink at him uncertainly, hoping his indulgent manner would not change.

Their table was reserved, a table for two, but no sooner had they sat down than Nickolas was hailed from a table close by. Marika could not understand what had been said, nor the reply from Nickolas, but the smile of pleasure on his face was easily interpreted.

'We'll join my friends.' he said, and they moved to the larger table.

The couple were Greek, Leonides and Niki Makris. Leonides was the captain of a cruise ship, now at anchor at Piraeus for a thirty-six hour stay. His home was in Corfu, but Niki had decided to join him when the ship docked at Piraeus, and continued the voyage with him. Obviously the two men were delighted to see one another, and when the Makrises learned who Marika was they fairly beamed on her.

'Nick to be married at last!' Niki, in true Greek fashion, reached across the table to pat Marika's arm affectionately. 'We had begun to despair, for he would never even look at a woman!'

Glancing swiftly at Nickolas, Marika met an impassive gaze. If he did have all those pillow friends, he would naturally keep the fact a secret, she supposed, and then another thought struck her. Some day he would have to admit his engagement was broken, and that, she felt, would not please him at all.

'If I remember, Leon kept his freedom much longer,' put in Nickolas suavely. 'Even your charms, Niki, did not tempt him.'

'How ungallant!' she pouted, though her dark eyes laughed. 'But I caught him in the end!' She picked up her glass, sipping the wine slowly. 'You all get caught in the end,' she went on. 'But with you, Nick, I think Marika has been very, very clever!'

Marika helped herself to a roll, and broke it with trembling fingers, then picked up her soup spoon. Never had she felt quite so embarrassed as this.

'You are making her blush,' Leon admonished with mock severity. 'Stop it!'

'English girls blush so easily – and yet it is – what—?' She turned to her husband, but he could not produce the word, either.

'Enchanting,' supplied Nickolas coolly. But Marika's growing discomfort touched him and he added, 'Ignore these two, my dear, their manners are appalling!'

They all laughed then, and the conversation became less personal, though Niki wanted to know how Marika came to possess one of the prettiest of Greek names.

'My father was very fond of Greece,' she submitted, smiling, 'and the people, too.'

'So he gave you a Greek name? How very nice that was.'

The dinner proved to be a most pleasant meal, full of light chatter, and soon Marika felt as if she had known this charming couple all her life. The Greeks just took you to their hearts, and there you remained. Surely no people in the world could be so friendly and sincere

Leon, incredibly handsome, was as tall as Nickolas, and as slender. Immaculate in his uniform, his tanned skin clear and tight, and his jet black hair brushed sleekly back from his forehead, he looked to Marika exactly as the captain of a pleasure ship should look. Romantic – and somehow quite out of reach.

She'd been trying to visualize the ship, the *Pandrosos* named after the goddess of the dew, and to imagine life on board, when suddenly the trend of conversation between Nickolas and Leon penetrated.

'We shall be back on Saturday morning. Of course you can spare the time, Nick.'

'And you have the cabins?'

'Yes, I can arrange for two first class cabins. Quite a number of passengers have left us this time at Piaeus – they do, you know. Not everybody takes the full cruise.' He smiled at Marika who, by this time, had begun to tremble, almost visibly, with excitement – and hope.

Nickolas seemed to be idly watching the wine in his glass, its changing colour as he moved it gently in the light. But he was in fact considering, his dark eyes thoughtful. He glanced at Marika, smiling faintly as he sensed her anticipation.

'I'll think about it,' he agreed at length, 'and let you know in the morning.'

'Do come,' urged Niki, aware of Marika's glowing expression. 'It won't be new to you, Nick, but Marika would love to do a little island-hopping.'

'Yes, I believe she would. However, I really must give it some thought, for I hadn't meant to be away from Father for more than two or three days.'

No. Marika had already thought of that, and her hopes had sunk instantly. She felt selfish for even considering the idea.

Leon and Niki were visiting friends, and after arranging to meet at breakfast the following morning, Nickolas and Marika set out to walk to the high knoll from which Nickolas said they would view the illuminated monuments of the Acropolis.

Nickolas had said she would remember it for a long time; Marika knew she would remember it for ever.

The still, balmy air; the crescent moon reflected in the bay of Piraeus, far below; Mount Lykabettus rising above Athens, crowned by a shining white chapel ... and the Acropolis, its temples subtly bathed in lights of sheer magic – rose and gold and white.

This was how Marika first saw the Acropolis, this was how Nickolas meant her to see it. She would always be grateful to him, grateful for a most beautiful memory that nothing could ever erase from her mind.

Nickolas stood so close that she felt he must surely sense the emotion which engulfed her, an emotion that deprived her of speech, that hurt so much she felt inexpressibly relieved when Nickolas said flippantly,

'Would you like my handkerchief?'

She laughed, then, and looked up at him, her eyes too bright.

'Nickolas ... you know how I feel?' She shook her head as if to throw off the spell. 'It's so beautiful, I can hardly bear it!' And she suddenly realized that he must be passionately fond of his city, ensuring as he did that she should first see it like this.

83

The haunting magic of the night, the softness and the warmth, encompassed them both, and it seemed quite natural for Nickolas to take her hand, to lead her gently to a little wooden seat, to pull her down beside him, still clasping her hand in his.

For a long while they sat under the stars, silent, for words seemed out of place. Then Nickolas, determined to make her day still more memorable, suggested they visit a night club.

They went to one of the more expensive tavernas in the Plaka, where they sat in a garden with vines for a roof, drank *retsina* and watched the folk dancing until one in the morning.

Back in the hotel, in Nickolas's luxurious sitting-room overlooking the lighted square, Marika sank into a chair, while Nickolas went into the bedroom, to collect what he required for the night. When he came out she was almost asleep.

'Wake up, you mustn't fall asleep in the chair!'

'No!' Startled, she came to, yawning. 'Thank you for a lovely day, Nickolas. . . .' Again she yawned. 'I think, after all, that I *am* cut out for the high-life.'

A soft laugh escaped him. He opened the door.

'I doubt it, my child. I doubt it very much.'

Marika awoke to the rattle of dishes close at hand, and the brilliant sun streaming through the window. Getting out of bed, she put on a dressing gown, combed her hair, then went to investigate.

Nickolas, sleeves rolled up, seemed to fill the tiny kitchen. Marika noticed the two glasses of fruit juice already on the tray, the jar of honey, the bottle of powdered coffee on the table by the stove. He had surprised her many times, but never so much as this. She had wondered about the kitchen on seeing it last evening, for Nickolas seemed the last person to do anything for himself, more especially as he had merely to press a bell to receive immediate attention. He was so absorbed that she had to give a slight cough before he turned, to examine her face critically.

'So you're up. How do you feel?'

'Fine.' She glanced again at the tray. 'Aren't we having breakfast with Leon and Niki?'

'I've just seen Leon; told him we'd be down later. I thought, somehow, that you wouldn't be feeling up to it.'

How considerate! And yet, at the same time, how unconcerned he appeared at seeing her standing there, in her bare feet, with sleep still pricking her eyes, making her blink too much.

Pillow friends. . . . Naturally he would not wish the hotel staff to know, and naturally he would give them breakfast. . . .

The idea hurt, in a way that puzzled her, and a shadow crossed her face.

'Are you sure you feel all right?' and then, inflexibly, 'Two glasses of wine only in future. You're not used to it.'

Her face cleared and she laughed, watching him with the coffee jar, and the spoon.

'I felt dizzy once or twice. It was lovely – like floating, and I didn't care what happened. It was a *beautiful* feeling, Nickolas!'

'I hope you made the most of it, for you won't feel like that again! Now, go and get dressed; breakfast's nearly ready.'

They had almost finished the meal when he asked her if she would like to see one or two of the islands. She put down her cup with a jerk and her eyes sparkled, but she said anxiously,

'Can we leave Father for so long?'

'We would be away four days. I think it would make him happy to know I was at last taking some interest in you.' For a brief space he looked troubled. 'He has made some odd remarks lately, as though. . . .' He tailed off, frowning as if at an unpleasant recollection. 'He mustn't ever guess, Marika— Have you noticed any doubt in his manner?'

'No, we talk about the future a lot. I'm sure he hasn't any idea that we're not really engaged.'

'Could be my imagination, I suppose.' Nickolas poured her some more coffee. 'I think we will take that trip, all the same. As I said before, you should see all you can while you have the opportunity.' He went on to say that Kostos could go up to Delphi, take some books which Stephanos wanted, and fetch Souphoula to stay for a few days. 'She will enjoy that, and Father cannot be lonely with his mother and Pitsa there to keep him entertained.'

As Nickolas had obviously made up his mind to join Leon's ship, Marika now found it impossible to curb her excitement.

'How many islands will we see? How long do we stay there? Is it a big ship?' Her eyes shone but, noticing the growing amusement on his face, she flushed and added, more soberly, 'Will we dine with Leon and Nikki?'

'We shall, I expect, sit at their table.'

Again Marika's eyes shone.

'Dining with the captain! It's like a fairy tale. Won't I have a lot to tell them when I get home!'

Silence dropped. Nickolas pushed a little bowl towards her and she helped herself to sugar. She noticed a muscle move in his neck, and a sudden tightness appear about his mouth. Her own throat felt dry. Nickolas said unexpectedly,

'Are you looking forward to going home, my child?'

Marika stirred her coffee, her brow furrowed in doubt.

'I don't know,' she admitted, trying to bring into focus the narrow village street, the dark mass of the forest spreading away in the background, and the stately Norman church and mediaeval inn. 'I shall always want to come back.'

86

'Naturally; Greece has stolen your heart, it always does. But with you the call will be stronger, for you have lived with us, intimately. My family love you and, I think, you love them. Is that not so?'

'Yes, I think your family are wonderful.' She fell silent, sipping her coffee. "Greece has stolen your heart". ... Indeed it had, but. ... She recalled that merciless embrace, that brutal kiss, and her own scared awakening. Her eyes flickered, met her fiancé's dark and penetrating gaze, and a vivid flush rose to her cheeks. All confusion, she stammered, 'Are you waiting for me? I've finished now – shall I help you with the dishes?'

They were to board the ship at about six that evening, Nickolas stated. In the meantime, they would spend the morning sightseeing, including a visit to the Acropolis, and discuss, later, how they would spend the afternoon. He intended leaving the car and using a taxi, and Marika felt pleased that he was having a complete change, even from driving. He went off to give Kostos his instructions, telling Marika to wait for him in the hotel entrance. But she went outside, intending to have a look round. Immediately she found herself approached by a taxi driver, smiling, and speaking in excellent English.

'You want a taxi?'

She smiled and shook her head, but then wondered if Nickolas had perhaps not yet arranged for their taxi.

'I don't know. Will you wait a little while?'

'You have a friend? Your friend comes with you?'

'Yes.' Her smile deepened as several other drivers approached. She felt in no way self-conscious, for she and Pitsa often chatted to the taxi men at Delphi.

'What part of England do you come from?' the first driver was asking, when his friend interrupted.

'I am from your country. Alexandros of Swansea!'

Marika's smile broadened. She'd been teased like this before.

'You've been in the Merchant Navy. That is why you've

been to Swansea.'

'The lady knows that you tell the one big lie, Alex.' The man was stocky, with toughened skin and a grin that spread to his dark eyes. 'I, now, I have been long time in the Merchant Navy. I go to Liverpool – you have been there?'

'I live not very far from there.'

'I go there for nineteen days—' He broke off, his face creasing with mock agony. 'It rain, and it rain, and it *rain*! For nineteen whole days it rain!'

Marika burst out laughing, and the men all joined in.

'That is an exaggeration; it never rains for nineteen days, even in Liverpool!'

'And in Swansea it rain,' put in Alex. 'How do you live with all that rain!'

'Here it rain for two-three months, and then. . . .' The stocky driver looked heavenwards, at the dazzling blue sky, with here and there the merest wisp of stratus cloud. 'We have it fine – always it is fine.'

Yes, indeed. The glorious sunshine, the certainty of fine weather. The outdoor cafés everywhere, and no one dreaming of taking anything in at night.

'No wonder you are all so happy,' she murmured, with a quick backward glance. Nickolas seemed to be taking a very long time.

'Happy? Yes.' Alex, taking a few drachmae from his pocket, rattled the coins in his hand. 'Poor, we are, but—' he, too gazed skywards, 'we are always happy because of the sun!'

Marika thought of all the people she knew at home, of their hurry and rush – striving for what? Money ... everything these days seemed to hinge on the race for money, the desire to go better than one's neighbour. She felt ashamed, and humble, and filled with admiration all at once.

'I think I must go and look for my friend,' she said at last. 'But wait, won't you? We might require your taxi.'

'Yanni will wait for you all the day!' he returned gallantly.

'Is your name really Yanni?' she wanted to know, eyeing him with sudden severity.

He looked hurt, turned to his friends for confirmation. 'I am Yanni? Yes.' They all nodded, obviously puzzled.

'I'm sorry,' she said hastily, and made to re-enter the hotel, but Yanni took hold of her arm.

'You want my taxi for the whole day?'

'Perhaps, but I will let you know in a few minutes.'

'It will be so hot in Athens this afternoon, and I have an idea.' Yanni's arm slipped in friendly fashion round her shoulders. 'I will take you and your friend to—'

Marika felt the arm removed, saw the other taxi men drift away.

'I wish, Yanni,' said Nickolas in acid tones, 'that you would confine your persuasive endeavours to words!'

Yanni gasped in astonishment.

'Mr. Loukas!' He glanced from Nickolas to Marika, and back again. 'You have found a lady friend – at last!'

No mistaking the meaning of that remark. Marika felt a warm glow inside her, but the happy smile faded as she looked up into her fiancé's austere countenance.

'What is this idea you have for this afternoon?' asked Nickolas, and Yanni shrugged, obviously disappointed.

'You have your car, Mr. Loukas.'

'We shall hire your taxi. I am not driving today,' he said, the coldness leaving his tones. 'We want to see the city before lunch, while it is comparatively cool. Tell us what you have in mind for later on?'

'Yesterday it was a hundred and ten in Athens – too hot!' Yanni turned to Marika, gesturing as if to wipe the perspiration from his brow. 'I will take you this afternoon to Cape Sounion. We find a quiet bay and you and Mr. Loukas make swimming. How is that!'

'Lovely!' exclaimed Marika impulsively. 'Can we do

that, Nickolas? I would like to make swimming!' Although her easy use of the Greek expression brought a faint smile to Nickolas's face, his eyes retained their censure.

'An excellent idea,' he told Yanni, opening the car door. 'You can take us to the shops first, then you can give us the usual tour.'

Nickolas bought her a swim-suit and a beach robe, then she asked if they could go into the souvenir shop; she wished to buy some small gifts to send home. She bought delicately embroidered cloths and mats for her mother and the twins, and a silver key ring for David.

She toyed with a silver ring for a while, debating on whether or not to get it for herself. Souphoula had insisted on giving her money to buy something for her own use, and Marika wanted to make sure that she bought something durable. The price had been dropped several times, as the shopkeeper endeavoured to make a sale. Marika could not bring herself to bargain with him after that.

'I'll have it,' she said, and put it on. It was hand-made, a 'seal' ring, with the head of Zeus encircled by laurel leaves. 'Do you like it?' She smiled up at Nickolas, who nodded, his glance on her wrist.

'I haven't seen you wearing a watch,' he said. 'Does that mean you don't possess one?'

'I left it at home – in England.' She did not add that it was one Susan had given her, or that it was broken.

'I must get you one,' he promised. 'We may find something nice on the ship.'

Leaving the taxi to make its way to the official entrance to the Acropolis, where Yanni was to wait for them, Nickolas and Marika climbed up through the old streets of the Plaka, reaching a great wall which completely hid the buildings above. Their way followed the contours of the wall, bringing them out to the north of the Propylaea.

They had met few people, for most of the tourists came by coach and were dropped by the hundreds on the terrace just below the steps of the Propylaea. Here were to be found the numerous pedlars with their miscellany of postcards, local handicrafts, sponges, and 'alabaster' models of the buildings of the Acropolis.

Marika had expected to approach the great rock from this direction, for Pitsa had described it to her, but once again Nickolas had wished her first impression to be the most favourable, and again she experienced that sense of gratitude, while at the same time wondering why he should take so much trouble.

As they mounted the steps, however, there was no escaping the mass of tourists, speaking a dozen languages, snapping endless cameras, following obediently in the wake of their perspiring, hoarse-throated guides.

But to Marika, coming through the massive gateway of the Propylaea, nothing could mar her first prospect of the ancient buildings, especially the Parthenon, the mighty temple to the goddess Athena. The original radiant white Pentelic marble had weathered to a warm golden ochre which gave an added beauty to the building which was universally acclaimed the most perfect example of Doric architecture in the world.

They walked in the temple, and Nickolas recounted some of the history of the sacred rock. He told her how Athena and Poseidon had vied for the patronage of the city, so strategically placed, protected as it was by a half-circle of mountains. Poseidon, with true male arrogance, had thrust his trident at the rocks, bringing forth a war-like steed, symbol of aggression, but the clever Athena, goddess of wisdom, brought forth an olive tree, symbol of peace. The gods of Olympus had decided in her favour and the city was re-named after her.

Marika, with loving hands, touched the fluted column, and although Nickolas appeared merely amused, she knew he was pleased. Like all Greeks, he possessed great pride in his heritage.

They then went to the Erechtheum, with its famous Porch of the Caryatids, where the actual contest between Athena and the sea god had taken place. Here the olive tree grew, and into this building fell the olive-wood statue of Athena, after its descent from heaven. In contrast to the noble Parthenon, the Erechtheum was graceful, delicate, built in the Ionic style like the enchanting little Temple of Athena Nike, standing on a projecting shelf close to the Propylaea.

Nickolas, with that new patience and gentleness which Marika found far more disturbing than his former arrogance, did not seem to mind how long she stared, or stood amid the ruins idly dreaming of a distant glorious past. He answered every question, expounded on the orders of architecture, told her of the endless wars, of the Turkish occupation, and still she thirsted for more.

'It is time to go,' he insisted at last. 'We shall come again, many times.' Something in the way he said that made her glance up quickly, but he revealed no emotion.

It was almost noon; the heat felt blistering, and the reflection of sunlight thrown back from the marble ruins became blinding when caught from certain angles. Reluctantly Marika agreed they should leave.

Merging with the throng, they made their way to where the coaches and taxis were parked, awaiting the return of the sightseers. Spotting them, Yanni waved. Marika, a smile spreading, waved gaily back – then wished she hadn't, for her action reminded Nickolas of something he had to say.

'What do you mean by allowing Yanni to pat and paw you?'

'He didn't— What a horrid word!' Marika turned her head indignantly, the colour rushing to her face. 'He'd never dream of – of pawing!'

'Do you think I don't know my own people?'

'Then you must understand they don't mean anything,' she pointed out reasonably. 'It's merely a gesture of affection. I think it's rather nice.'

'Indeed.' His tones were frigid. 'You surprise me, Marika!' And then, 'I will not have Yanni – or anyone else – fondling you – whether you enjoy it or not!'

CHAPTER SIX

His words remained with Marika for a very long time; through the drive back to the hotel, through lunch, and the drive to Cape Sounion.

She had seen Nickolas in many moods during the past couple of months; he had been arrogant, sinister, amused, indulgent. He had many times been impatient of her slips made with Stephanos; had been indifferent, often to the point of forgetting her presence altogether . . . but not once had he displayed that imperious, possessive attitude of this morning.

'*I* will not have Yanni . . . fondling you.'

The words were somehow linked with those of Souphoula. She had said it was a good thing Marika was not really engaged to Nickolas, otherwise she'd find herself in trouble.

He could not be – *could* not be— Marika found it almost impossible to form the word 'jealous' even vaguely in her mind.

She wondered if he really were in love with Hilary. She knew he had an affection for her; it had been apparent in his eyes, in his manner and in the way he paid her little attentions.

Nickolas, it seemed, had forgotten all about those words which Marika found so troublesome, for he chatted to her over lunch, and on the way to Sounion he several times included Yanni in the conversation. They stopped at a little café for refreshments, drinking *ouzo* and taking the *mezé* that usually went with it. Then they walked up to the ruins of the Temple of Poseidon, and later found a deserted bay which they managed to keep to themselves for the rest of the afternoon.

Nickolas and Yanni walked away, chatting, while

Marika changed in the car, then she waited, sitting on the warm shingle, until Nickolas, having changed, came to join her. They swam together for some time, and then Nickolas went far out, as if wishing to be alone. Marika felt a strange content and joy that he could relax like this, forget his work, and even the sadness of his father's health for a while.

After playing about on her own she came out of the water – and because those words again intruded, she picked up her beach coat and wrapped it around her before joining Yanni, who was sitting on a rocky ledge, playing with worry beads and looking placidly out to sea.

She sat down opposite to him, watching his fingers with the beads. That inherent tactility could be discerned in every movement.

'Don't you ever get bored, Yanni?' she asked after a while, for he still gazed out to sea, as if his thoughts were far away.

'Bored? No, why should I get bored?'

'Bringing tourists out every day. Surely you must tire of it sometimes.'

'I am lucky. The visitors like to come to the sea, and I come to the sea, also. And I sit here like this, and get paid for it – paid for doing nothing!'

'But do you get well paid?' she wanted to know. 'I mean, people always bargain with you, knock down your price.'

'The pay is good.' Yanni grinned broadly. 'We like to bargain, you know, just as much as they. Sometimes it gets – heated, and sometimes people want too much knocked off, and then we are insulted.' He looked grave, and rather pained. 'A fair price we want – and always the English give us a fair price, because they very much like to make harmony. In Greece we think the English are very good.'

Marika felt warm at hearing this, and happy. The

affection in her eyes was not particularly for Yanni, but for all the Greeks she had met. She did not know it was still in her eyes as Nickolas came up, but she did know that as she looked up at him, smiling, his own eyes flickered oddly before he said, in the gentlest tones he had ever used to her,

'Come and make swimming with me for another few minutes – and then we must go.'

But when they came out of the water they joined Yanni, who had found a sandy part of the beach, and sat for a while, drying themselves in the sun.

'Everything is so vivid, so beautifully clear,' she remarked, her eyes moving slowly from the waves, frothing gently at her feet, to the countless islands that had not been visible from any other place she had visited.

'At Sounion it is always like this,' Nickolas told her. 'The air is exceptionally clear, and that, combined with the brilliance of the sun, brings out the colours of the sea, and of the land.'

A few hours later they were on the deck of the *Pandrosos*, watching the sun falling quickly behind Salamis. Here again, the colours charmed her, delicate gold changing to a deep amethyst, bathing the island in that magical, almost supernatural light which she had first noticed on entering Athens.

The deck was crowded, for it was the height of the season; all were dressed for dinner, all awaiting the summons to the restaurant.

The meal was a lively affair, with lights and laughter and the babble of many tongues. Someone had a birthday; a cake was carried the length of the dining-room with the orchestra following, playing 'Happy Birthday'. Everyone clapped and cheered noisily as the cake was presented.

Marika tasted her first caviar, drank her first champagne. She became fascinated by the large, deep-throated American woman, flashing incredible dia-

Your special introduction to the Mills & Boon Reader Service.
A chance to enjoy 4 spellbindin; Romances absolutely FREE.

Four exciting Mills & Boon Romances have been specially selected for you to enjoy FREE and without any obligation. You can meet Carolir her imminent marriage threatened by a misunderstanding . . . Karen, forced to meet the husband she still loves two years after their divorce . . Sabrina, tragically blinded and fighting a little too hard to be independer . . . Ravena, about to marry a forbidding stranger to protect her beloved guardian from a terrible secret.

Intriguing relationships . . . memorable characters . . . exciting locations . . . Our readers tell us that the books we select have them 'hooked' from the very first page. And they're a joy to read to the last loving embrace.

The Unwilling Bride
by Violet Winspear
Ravena loved her guardian and desperately wanted to protect him fro terrible secret about his son. But that meant marrying forbidding Mark di Curzio in order to bear him a son.

The Marriage of Caroline Lindsay
by Margaret Rome
Caroline agreed to marry Domenico Vicari to give her sister's abandoned baby a home and security. But Domenico believed the baby to be Caroline's own.

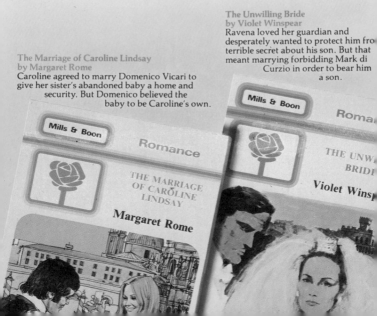

Mills & Boon

Romance

THE MARRIAGE OF CAROLINE LINDSAY

Margaret Rome

Mills & Boon

Roma

THE UNW BRID

Violet Wins

With the help of the Mills & Boon Reader Service you could receive
very latest Mills & Boon titles hot from the presses each month. And
can enjoy many other exclusive
antages:

No commitment. You receive books for only as long as you want.

No hidden extra charges. Postage and packing is free.

Friendly, personal attention from Reader Service Editor, Susan
land. Why not ring her now on 01-689 6846 if you have any queries?

FREE monthly newsletter crammed with knitting patterns, recipes,
petitions, bargain book offers, and exclusive special offers for you,
r home and your friends.

FOUR FREE BOOKS ARE OUR SPECIAL GIFT TO YOU. THEY ARE
URS TO KEEP WITHOUT ANY OBLIGATION TO BUY FURTHER BOOKS.

have nothing to lose—and a
le world of romance to gain.
fill in and post the coupon
ay.

s & Boon Reader Service,
Box 236, Croydon, Surrey CR9 9EL.

Ivory Cane
net Dailey
ina coped bravely with the tragedy of
g blinded in an accident. But how could
she cope with a man who offered pity
when she needed his love?

Seen by Candlelight
by Anne Mather
Even two years after their divorce, Karen
still loved her husband Paul. To protect
her sister from the advances of Paul's
married brother Karen must meet him
again—a meeting she
dreaded.

Mills & Boon
Romance

THE IVORY
CANE
Janet Dailey

Mills & Boon
Romance

SEEN BY
CANDLELIGH
Anne Mathe

See overleaf for your
FREE BOOKS
order form.

monds, by the French girl with several beaux in tow, by the English lady who sighed nostalgically,

'This food! What I would give for a plate of bacon and eggs!'

Leon and Niki teased her about not eating.

'I'm too excited,' she confessed naively. 'I haven't ever been on a ship before.'

Niki gazed at her curiously, then looked at Nickolas. 'I guess you haven't seen much at all. Nick tells us that you had never been far from your little village?'

'I hadn't. But I've seen ever such a lot since coming to Greece. I never thought I'd be as lucky as this.' She smiled at Nickolas who, after allowing his eyes to rest reflectively on her for a moment, smiled in return.

'You're so appreciative, my dear. You make me feel quite guilty.'

After dinner they danced, watched a fancy dress competition, then danced again. Marika felt scared when Leon asked her to dance, because everyone's eyes invariably followed the handsome captain whenever he stepped on to the floor. Fortunately it was so crowded that any mistakes she made passed unnoticed.

And owing to the lack of space Nickolas had several times to pull her close in order to avoid colliding with other couples. She felt his heart strongly beating against her cheek; his nearness became too disturbing and she sighed with relief when he said,

'This heat's overpowering; let us see what it's like outside.'

They went on deck, but even there the air remained still, and soft as down. Nickolas stopped by the rail and they stood gazing over the side as the vessel skimmed gracefully over the winking waves. The moon shed little light, but the Aegean's placid waters shone with a strange lambency, as if possessed of some inner force of light harvested from the super brilliance of the day. Overhead a million stars hung in a velvet sky with the

97

crescent moon suspended in their midst. With magic all around her, and the heady sensation of being poised on the brink of eternity, Marika's heart swelled with gratitude for these memories that Nickolas had given her. Impulsively she laid a hand upon his arm and murmured, in tones as gentle as the night,

'Efaristo poli.'

A star shot across the sky and dropped over the rim of the world.

'Do not thank me,' he returned. 'I happen to be enjoying this, too.' And his hand covered hers, enclosing it in a way that sent her pulses racing. She said, in the haste of confusion,

'But you have been before, many times – and the dancing, and the noise – I shouldn't have thought they would appeal to you.'

He listened for a moment to the sound of music floating out to them from the open windows of the night club.

'It depends on the company.' He spoke with infinite gentleness, and at the same time his clasp on her hand tightened, as if in anticipation of its sudden withdrawal. Marika, contained in a powerful emotion, could not trust herself to speak. Fleetingly she thought of David, and the quiet pleasure of holding his hand. But this . . . this was sheer ecstasy!

How long they stood there she did not know. She and Nickolas were detached from time. It had no meaning in this enchanted realm where heaven seemed to beckon, just a dream away.

And in that silent interlude they each beheld the truth – and each was conscious of a momentary fear.

The ship anchored off Delos, and they reached the island by launch. Nickolas asked if she wished to go along with the guide; Marika shook her head and they waited until the crowd had drifted away.

With the new happiness that had entered into her, Marika's eyes took on an added brightness, and her cheeks glowed as she smilingly informed him that he was to be her guide.

He had last been there in the spring, when flowers grew in wild profusion among the sacred ruins.

'We must come in the spring some day,' he said, quite naturally, as if there were now no possibility of her leaving Greece.

He took her hand as they strolled amid the ruins of Apollo's temple, and his sister's sanctuary. They walked along the Processional Way, with the famous row of marble lions gazing down from a small terrace above, climbed steps to the summit of Mount Cynthos, from where they could see the surrounding circle of islands, gems in indigo sea.

The sun blazed down on the tiny, barren island, once so holy, so filled with the purity of Apollo, whose birthplace it was, that no one was permitted to be born or to die there. Later, though covering a mere two square miles, it became an important centre of commerce, and the lovely villas built by the wealthy merchants and bankers provided some of the most fascinating monuments. Still bright with painted stucco, their floors were paved with delicate mosaics, after which the houses were often named. In the House of the Masks were the masks of five actors, and an elaborate mosaic of Dionysus riding a panther. In the house of Dionysus the handsome god of ecstasy rode a tiger. There were many others, the House of the Trident, the House of the Dolphins, and several archaic temples to be visited before they at last left the island and returned to the ship for lunch.

The afternoon was spent on Mykonos, the fairy-tale island of sandy hills floating on a sea of deepest blue, of glistening white houses and churches and windmills. The only colour allowed was on doors and shutters, and on the roofs and cupolas of the churches. These made a vivid contrast to the dazzling whiteness, and the inhabitants also grew numerous flowers in pots, hibiscus and oleanders, splashing scarlet and pink on to the whitewashed walls and shining marble steps.

The following day they landed by small launch at Skala, the port of Patmos, and long before they sailed away Marika knew that, no matter how much of Greece she was fated to see in her lifetime, this would always remain her dream island.

Volcanic and arid, with rugged coves and deep inlets, it still possessed that softness and warmth, that sublime quality of peace and remoteness which she had encountered where ever she went. Like a priceless jewel it rested on a bed of blue velvet, with that incredible Grecian sky as a cover.

After stopping in the square for refreshments, they went with the throng to climb up to the Byzantine monastery built over the spot where St. John was reputed to have written the Book of Revelations. Most people went by donkey, but Nickolas and Marika preferred to walk. On the way along the rocky ascent they were approached by a charming Greek child, dark, with a clear skin and all the classical features of a young goddess. Smiling, she held out a flower to Marika.

'Will you have my flower?' The child could not have been more than four or five, yet she spoke in English, with a beautiful deep-toned accent.

'Thank you very much!' Marika, thrilled, took the flower from her hand and put it in the buttonhole of her blouse, watching the pleasure sparkle in the child's eyes. '*Efaristo.*'

Nickolas had his hand in his pocket. The child shyly took the drachmae offered.

'*Efaristo,*' she said, and was off like a shot into the doorway of a low, whitewashed house a few yards ahead.

'She – was begging?'

'Afraid so.' Nickolas glanced at Marika in some amusement. 'Disappointed?'

Marika hesitated, fingering the fragrant petals.

'No, I don't think so. Only the Greeks could beg like that – with such dignity.'

He laughed then, and his voice was almost tender.

'I do believe you'd forgive us anything!'

'Yes, I believe I would.' She saw the child reappear, with a flower in her hand, and smiled faintly to herself.

'I shall remember that,' said Nickolas, and although his tones were light she sensed a depth of meaning in the words.

They had reached a small roadside café; through the open door came the strains of Greek folk music played by *bouzouki* and a guitar. Marika had to stop and watch for a moment the three men leaping and bending with amazing grace and agility. They appeared to be workmen, or local inhabitants who, having gone into the café for refreshments, had taken the floor merely as a diversion.

The 'orchestra' were sitting along one wall; old, weatherbeaten men with deeply lined faces and the inevitable hint of humour and goodwill in their eyes. The guitarist beckoned to them to come inside, speaking in Greek. Nickolas replied, then took Marika's arm and they continued on their way up to the monastery.

Marika began to speak, trying to hide her disappointment, but Nickolas interrupted her.

'I promised we would call in on our way back,' he said. 'We shall then know how much time we have. Mustn't keep the ship waiting.'

The café was crowded with visitors when they came down again, and they could not find seats. The guitarist, recognizing them, called to Marika to choose some music.

With a questioning glance at Nickolas, who nodded, she went over to the old man, asking for, 'Never on Sunday'. He smiled, spoke to the others, and they began to play.

Almost immediately several young Greek girls and men got up to dance, laughingly indicating their wish for some of the visitors to join in.

'I can't do it,' said Marika hastily as one girl grabbed her arm.

'They are willing to teach you,' Nickolas informed her as he, too, was dragged into the circle.

They danced with arms entwined; the visitors all made mistakes at first, but no one cared. Never had Marika felt so happy, so completely abandoned. Everyone laughed, and hummed the tune or sang the words. Over and over the tune was played; eventually Nickolas managed to put himself next to Marika.

'We must go,' he warned. 'The ship sails at one o'clock.'

'Can't we stay just a little while longer?' For one mad, intoxicated moment she wished the ship would sail without them, wished they could stay here like this for ever.

'No, I'm afraid not.' His voice held a note of inflexibility, and with a little sigh of resignation, Marika left the circle of dancers and followed him to the door.

'*Kalí andámosi!*' called the young men and girls, waving gaily, while continuing the dance.

'*Kalí andámosi,*' returned Nickolas, while Marika added, rather bleakly,

'Good-bye.'

'*Au revoir,*' corrected Nickolas softly as they stepped into the brilliant sunshine. 'We shall come back, my dear.'

'Will we, Nickolas?' She looked up as they hurried along, her eyes pleading, almost desperate. 'Will we ever come back, do you think?'

'Haven't I said so? Certainly we shall come back, many times.' Despite his apparent confidence, he seemed unsure, in fact, Marika had the strange impression that he was not very sure about anything.

But the feeling soon passed, for he took her hand, because the path was rough and stony; two Orthodox priests, on their way to the monastery, smiled faintly. A greeting passed between them and Nickolas, and then their lips moved silently, as if in blessing.

Nickolas and Marika continued on their way, meeting men with laden donkeys, women selling exquisite embroidery set out on rough stalls by the roadside, their brown skins toughened and wrinkled by the merciless sun.

'Do you want anything?' asked Nickolas, slowing down his hitherto rapid pace.

'I would like a souvenir, if we have time.'

He bought her an embroidered cloth, conversing with the smiling woman first. Had he bargained? She hoped not; the poverty of these people hurt her.

'How do they live?' she wanted to know, for obviously there would be times when the island was without tourists, and scarcely anything grew on that parched and stony land.

'Mainly by sponge-fishing. The men dive for them.' He seemed faintly amused. 'You worry too much about people. They're happy with the sea and sky and God's sunshine—' He paused, steering her away from some fallen boulders strewn across their path. 'The Greeks may be poor, my dear, but they have their values right; you have no need to pity them.'

Yes, they had their values right. Not for them the futile striving, the greed and soul-destroying lust for something better. They were in fact to be envied, for they knew the true meaning of contentment.

Despite Nickolas's haste, they were the last to board the launch. As it moved from the quay, making for the gleaming white ship anchored just off the island, Marika looked back, a sad and lingering regret in her heart.

Would they ever return? Nickolas had said they would, and yet. . . . Something had happened to her during the past few days, and she suspected Nickolas felt differently, too, but try as she would, Marika could not visualize a future with him, could not help comparing herself with Hilary who was so beautiful, so confident and, perhaps more important, a clever and efficient businesswoman. No doubt at all that Nickolas relied on her a good deal, in fact, thought Marika with a tiny sigh, he would probably be lost without her.

The afternoon was spent on deck, under a blazing sun. Marika had acquired a beautiful tan – she looked almost like a Greek herself, Niki had laughingly told her when, after lunch, she joined them for a while. She had had her hair done during the morning while Nickolas and Marika were exploring Patmos and, noticing how attractive it looked, Marika said,

'I think I will have mine cut. Must I make an appointment?'

'Yes; she's rather busy, but I'll see you're fitted in.'

Nicholas, lying in a deck chair, apparently dozing, opened his eyes.

'Your hair suits you very well as it is,' he said quietly, and closed his eyes again, as if considering the matter settled.

'Oh. . . .' Marika appeared faintly surprised. 'Perhaps, but I've decided to have it short. And I might have it permed a little – just to make it curl up at the ends.'

Her fiancé's eyes opened very wide at that; Niki looked from him to Marika, and waited. Having known Nickolas a long time, she knew what that expression portended.

'Perhaps you did not understand me. I said your hair suits you as it is.'

Marika blinked at him, and flushed slightly, conscious of Niki's amusement.

'You mean you don't want me to have it cut?'

'He means,' laughed Niki, 'that he won't allow you to have it cut,' and, as a slight frown crossed Marika's brow,

'This is something you will have to get used to. Don't you know that in Greece, when the bride, during the marriage service, promises to obey, the bridegroom stamps heavily on her toes to remind her of his superiority?' She was laughing, and Nickolas himself seemed a good deal amused as he watched Marika's colour deepen.

'Those antiquated customs exist now only in the remote villages – Pitsa told me!' she retorted. 'If Nickolas stamped on my toes I'd—' She broke off, in utter confusion.

'You would stamp on mine?' responded Nickolas, laughter in his eyes. 'In that case, I had better take care, hadn't I?'

Perhaps that was merely for Niki's benefit; perhaps he was teasing her – or it could have been something of both. But it so added to Marika's embarrassment that, taking pity on her, Nickolas reluctantly left his chair and suggested they take a dip in the pool.

There remained to them two more idyllic days. On the first, they visited Rhodes, the 'island of roses', where they had a meal in one of the *tavernas* by the sea, strolled along the famous 'Street of the Knights', and visited the valley of the butterflies. They stood on one of the little rustic bridges and looked down into the gorge as the butterflies, disturbed by the visitors, showered the air with a deep crimson gold. They wandered into the Turkish town, with its markets and fountains, its slender minarets and mosque of Suleiman the Magnificent.

And on their last day they visited Crete, and the Palace of Minos at Knossos, with its beautiful frescoes, still bright after three thousand years. Here began Europe's first civilization; here the terrible monster, the Minotaur, was born to the wife of King Minos, and later slain by Theseus, legendary Prince of Athens.

'What a lot we've done!' said Marika as, after their last dinner on board, they left the dancers and strolled on the deck. 'I feel I've been away from Delphi for weeks!'

'Have you enjoyed it all?' The gentleness in his tone had become familiar, but Marika caught her breath on hearing it. They paused by the rail and she turned to him, her eyes wide and soft, her lips parted in a smile.

'I've had a wonderful time; I'll never, never forget it!'

'Nor shall I.' His voice held a hint of regret, as if he wished their holiday could have lasted a while longer. 'I hope, my dear, that I have in some small measure made up for my inexcusable neglect of you.'

Small measure! Fingering the watch on her wrist, thinking of her luxurious cabin, and the shore trips they had taken, Marika felt tempted to thank him again, but she refrained.

This holiday was just a more elaborate example of the hospitality found everywhere in Greece. Already she knew enough about the Greeks to be sure that Nickolas would not appreciate gratitude on her part. His regret at what he called his neglect was very sincere; what he had done for her both assuaged his conscience and gave him that self-fulfilment which requires no other reward.

Several couples came out on deck, escaping from the excessive heat of the ballroom, but it was an airless night, with scarcely a ripple on the sea, and Marika felt that the only comfortable place would be in the pool. On nights like this the air-conditioning helped, but the cabins were almost unbearably hot, and Marika knew that if she went to bed she wouldn't sleep. Nickolas seemed to have the same conviction, for he suggested they go up on to the top deck, and sit down for a while.

They sat there a long while, speaking little, but in the softness of the night the sense of companionship grew steadily. Marika recalled Elaine's saying that wonderful things happened to you in Greece. Well, something very wonderful had happened to her. Had something wonderful happened to Nickolas? She felt sure it had, and the knowledge set her wondering, with an almost ecstatic expectation, when, and how, he would tell her about it.

It was two in the morning before Nicholas said, with obvious reluctance, that it was time they were in their beds.

Back on the lower deck, they paused for a moment by the rail, watching the lights of another cruise ship away in the distance.

'It's like something out of fairyland,' Marika said, rather huskily, and then, 'Nothing seems *real*!'

'Nothing?' Gently he took her face between his hands, turning it up, to kiss her soft, quivering lips. 'Nothing except this—' He kissed her again, exulting as, after the first timid hesitancy, her lips grew responsive under his own and he knew the sweet joy of their freshness and warmth.

CHAPTER SEVEN

MARIKA was shocked by the change in Stephanos. She stood by the bed for a long moment, unable to speak. More flesh seemed to have wasted away from his cheeks, his eyes were paler than ever, and one hand lay tightly clenched on the bed cover.

'Ah, my daughter. . . .' His voice was slurred and scarcely audible. 'Where is Nickolas?'

'He's bringing in the luggage; he won't be long.' She sat down on the bed, took up his hand and placed it against her face.

'We shouldn't have left you, Father. How do you feel?'

Stephanos did not answer that and she wondered if he had heard.

'You look well, little one. Tell me all about it – what have you seen?'

'So many things.' Even in her sadness the memories gave her eyes a sparkle, and her voice an animation that brought a faint smile of satisfaction to the old man's thin, colourless lips. 'Athens first – oh, Athens!'

'Do not try to expound,' he said, letting his fingers caress her cheek. 'Others, more gifted, have failed.'

'Then the islands. Kostos told you about us going with Leon, of course?'

He nodded weakly.

'The meeting was most opportune. Which islands did you see?'

She told him all that had happened, pausing now and then, anxious lest she should tire him. But he seemed avid for a full account of what they had done, and when she had finished speaking he sighed contentedly, and as his hand again came to rest on the bed it lay there lightly, and unclenched. Marika frowned, recalling

Nickolas's remark about noticing some element of doubt in his father's manner. Right at the beginning Nickolas had stressed the need for care, had warned her that his father, despite his illness, was still very acute.

'Nickolas has made you happy, my little one.' The old man smiled, though his words came with an effort. Marika's heart lurched; she knew he was dreadfully ill. 'There is love in your eyes now,' he observed, looking at her intently. 'That was not so before you went away—' Marika made as if to protest, willing to attempt a convincing lie, but the old man found the strength to lift his hand. Yet he did not immediately continue; he stared past her, appearing to be lost in thought. 'I do not know what has been happening, but it seems that everything is all right now.'

So he had suspected, in spite of their caution! Marika dropped her hands to her lap, clasping them together so he should not notice their trembling. With a gasp of relief she heard the door open, and turned to cast Nickolas a warning glance which only served to puzzle him.

His father lay with closed eyes, but roused himself and moved his head on the pillow as Nickolas crossed the floor and stood by the bed, staring down at the waxen face intently.

'Father. . . .' He drew up a chair and sat down beside the bed facing Marika. 'You seem rather tired. What have you been doing?' He glanced at the pile of books on the table. 'Too much reading wearies you; you mustn't do it.'

'I shan't have to now.' He looked with affection at Marika, who smiled warmly in return. 'The little one will do it for me.'

'Yes, indeed, I will,' she promised, 'just whenever you wish me to.'

'Has the doctor been today?' asked Nickolas, smoothing the bedclothes with an apparently careless gesture.

The ghost of a smile touched the old man's lips.

'He has, yes. But what can the doctor do, my son?'

Nickolas flinched; he looked across at Marika, saw her fighting tears that threatened.

'What did he say?'

'What could he say? He has long since given up trying to hoax me.' His eyes narrowed, searching his son's face intently. 'I may be done for, Nickolas, but my brain's still active.'

'Indeed it is,' Nickolas calmly agreed. 'Dr. Moundanos would not be so unwise as to try to deceive you ... nor would anyone else who was acquainted with your almost uncanny—' He frowned, searching for the English word, and casting an inquiring glance at Marika. 'Omniscience – is that right, darling?'

Marika nodded, her eyes tender, her face softly glowing.

The old man's lids came down; he smiled faintly to himself, as if enjoying some secret joke. Then he said strangely,

'Queer how things turn out sometimes.' His head turned into the pillow; he seemed exhausted. 'My only regret is that I shall not live to see you married. Nickolas, there is a glass of water there on the table. Give it to me, please, and tell Pitsa I do not wish for tea – I'll have something later.'

Nickolas had to ease his father's head from the pillow, supporting it with his arm. Marika blinked swiftly as she watched him put the glass to the old man's lips. Stephanos had been more than capable of doing little things like that for himself before they went away. How different he had become – and in less than a week.

'Nickolas—' She turned to him and looked up into his face searchingly. 'Is he – will he . . .?'

A flicker of emotion crossed his face as, with infinite gentleness, he drew her closer to him.

'Could be a few weeks, I suppose,' he returned through tight lips. 'But, my dear, we must be prepared to lose him any time now.'

Marika wept on his breast; he held her in silence, his face caressing her hair. At last she pulled away, found a handkerchief and dried her eyes.

'You grew to love him too much,' Nickolas said sadly. 'It is always dangerous to love like that – you become so vulnerable to pain.' They had reached the top of the stairs. Marika stopped to examine his face again, wondering why her heartbeats should have quickened so madly. His warning referred to her affection for his father, and yet she felt there was a far deeper and more significant meaning to his words. Perhaps it was imagination. It *must* be imagination, she told herself in sudden fear, and because she felt so overwrought, the tears came again.

'What is it, my little one? Is it something else besides Father?' He impelled her towards his bedroom. 'Come in here and tell me all about it. In any case,' he added with a forced smile, 'you cannot go downstairs looking like this; they'll be wanting to know what I've been doing to you.' Closing the door, he turned her round; his anxiety was plain – and so was his tenderness.

'I'm so silly—' She managed to smile through her tears. 'The stupidest notion came into my head.'

'What stupid notion?' Nickolas took the wet little ball from her hand, held it gingerly for a moment, then put it on a chair. Drawing a handkerchief from his pocket he dried her eyes, then kissed her gently on the lips. 'Tell me about this stupid notion.'

With all her fears so quickly dispelled, she glanced up at him sheepishly. Her eyes were wide, and still glistening, her lips softly parted. Love had brought a delicate beauty to her childish features, though she had no idea why Nickolas caught his breath as he looked at her, waiting for her to speak. His hands on her bare arms trembled slightly, though their touch remained infinitely gentle.

'Everything is all right now,' she murmured. 'I felt –
frightened for a moment, but only because I was so upset about Father.'

'Death is frightening to the very young. But Father
has been resigned for some time. Undoubtedly he will
welcome it.' Nickolas gazed down at her steadily. 'The
important thing is that his last months have been made
happy, thanks to you, Marika. You have fulfilled your
role most successfully.'

He had obviously misunderstood the reason for her
fear, and she let that pass, but his comment on her
'success' reminded her of his father's doubts.

'He had guessed that all was not as it appeared,' she
admitted. 'It must have been something I did – but he is
quite happy now, and satisfied that we are – that I
am. . . .' Marika tailed off, flushing hotly. 'He had just
mentioned it before you came in. I tried to warn you, but
I don't think you understood my glance.'

A slight frown appeared on Nickolas's dark brow. He
seemed faintly troubled.

'Mentioned what?'

'He said he didn't know what had been happening,
but that he knew everything was all right now.' She
paused, watching his frown deepen, and realized she had
not, after all, completely lost her fear of him. 'He's quite
happy, Nickolas, truly,' she added in haste.

'Yes,' agreed Nickolas, diverted for the moment by
her still heightened colour. 'You have managed to dispel
any doubts he may have had.' He slid his fingers through
her hair, sweeping it back from her face as if to examine
her expression more closely. 'Father could not possibly
suspect anything now.' Marika blinked at him, conscious
of the warmth of his hand on her temple, and recalling
Stephanos's comment about the love in her eyes. Did her
face really reflect all that was in her heart? – Was that
what Nickolas had meant just now? She did not mind
if he knew how she felt about him, but – Oh, *when* would

he set her mind at rest by telling her of his feelings, too! His hand dropped and the frown reappeared. He went on to say that his father, having begun to suspect something, had probably been worrying while they were away, and that could have contributed to his worsening condition. 'On the other hand,' he continued in a voice faintly tender, 'if we hadn't gone away you wouldn't be looking so happy, and it is your obvious happiness that has set his fears at rest . . . once and for all, let us hope.'

There were others who noticed Marika's new-found happiness, and reacted to it in very different ways.

Souphoula had not yet gone back to her cottage, and she and Hilary were talking in the sitting-room when Nickolas and Marika came down. Marika had, on entering the house, merely popped her head round the door in greeting, then sped upstairs to see Stephanos, so neither woman had noticed the glow in her cheeks or the sparkle in her eyes.

Somehow, Souphoula had managed to find a high-backed, most uncomfortable-looking chair, and she sat on it, erect and unsmiling, her hands clasped together. She wore the usual full black skirt, and from beneath the black cowl a stray wisp of hair joined the numerous lines of her brow. Pitsa had once said that Souphoula knew the secret of the Evil Eye, and indeed she looked fearsome and terrible, and yet so very wise. She watched as Marika sat down on a small sofa, making room so that Nickolas could sit beside her if he wished. No flicker of expression touched Souphoula's face, but her black eyes seemed to penetrate Marika's very soul.

'Your holiday has done you good, child,' she observed, though her eyes flickered strangely as her grandson crossed the room and took a seat next to Hilary. 'You must come and see me tomorrow. I wish to know all about it.'

'Yes, I will,' Marika promised happily. 'We had a wonderful time, but I missed you all. Where's Pitsa?'

'Preparing her uncle's tea.' She paused. 'You will have noticed your father's condition?' she added, casting a glance at Nickolas.

He merely nodded, and continued his conversation with Hilary.

'Stephanos doesn't want tea.' Marika stood up, her eyes clouding in faint puzzlement at her fiancé's behaviour. 'I'll go and tell Pitsa – it's no use her getting it ready only to be wasted.'

'Uncle Stephanos is very ill,' Pitsa said when Marika gave her the message. 'He does not eat much at all now.' After a little reflective silence Pitsa added, more brightly, 'You look lovely, Marika. What havé you done to yourself?'

'Nothing at all, but we've had such a marvellous time, Pitsa. I adore your country!'

'Your country, too,' was the quick reminder. 'But it is not Greece that gives you this beauty. You have had a romantic time with Nickolas?'

Marika nodded, her eyes dreamy. She had to swallow a little lump in her throat before she could speak.

'Yes, Pitsa, it was romantic – the sea and the ship, and the islands. . . .' She added to herself, '. . . and Nickolas, so different, so tender and kind.' She felt happy that she no longer had to deceive her friend; it had hurt Marika to do so, and had hurt her even more to think of their parting.

Anna was at the other end of the room, preparing the tea tray. She never spoke much, always seeming to be immersed in her own thoughts, but she, too, remarked on Marika's changed appearance.

'You look very well, miss. The sea gives you good health – every time the sea is good for the health.'

Marika smiled at this, thanking her. She and Pitsa helped to carry in the tea things and set them out on the table. Nickolas brought up a coffee table and Pitsa put his and Hilary's tea on that, pouring out for them and passing the scones, which Hilary had made, and the typical sweet pastries that Pitsa had bought from the village confectioner's. Souphoula never took tea, but she drank several tiny cups of Turkish coffee, which Marika carried to her, for she never left her chair.

After tea Souphoula asked Nickolas to drive her home; Pitsa had already gone upstairs to spend half an hour with her uncle, so Marika found herself alone with Hilary.

The older girl had merely nodded in reply to Marika's quick greeting, and had scarcely spoken to her since. But the glances she cast at Marika could scarcely be ignored. From the first Marika had sensed her dislike, but those glances portrayed something far deeper. They had come at intervals, during her conversation with Nickolas; Marika could not even guess at the reason for them, because both Hilary and Nickolas had kept their voices so low that no one else in the room could hear what they said. Marika had felt a small ache of jealousy, especially as his eyes still held the old affection as he talked to Hilary, his head very close to hers.

Languidly, Hilary relaxed in her chair, staring at Marika from under thick, curling lashes.

'As Souphoula, in her great wisdom remarked, your holiday has done you good.' Always that half-sneer, thought Marika, and then wondered if she were being uncharitable.

'I do feel better for the holiday,' was all she said, thinking of Pitsa and Stephanos upstairs, and wishing she had been quick enough to join them before Souphoula and Nickolas went out.

'I suppose you were quite thrilled with the ship – after never having been anywhere before?'

'The sailing was enjoyable,' Marika replied, determined not to enter into details. Those hours on deck were far too precious to be discussed with anyone – except Nickolas himself.

'Poor Nick, he must have been frightfully bored!'

'He didn't appear to be bored,' retorted Marika with a toss of her head. 'In fact, I'm sure he thoroughly enjoyed every minute, just as I did.'

The colour fused Hilary's cheeks, so slowly that it was scarcely noticeable; Marika sensed, rather than saw, her anger.

'Naturally he wouldn't let you see his boredom,' she drawled, daintily tapping a manicured finger on the arm of her chair. 'You should know something about Greek ways by now. However fed up Nick was he'd have the good manners not to show it.'

'I don't believe he was in any way bored – or fed up as you say,' returned Marika with conviction. 'Nickolas is not the sort of person to have gone had he not expected to enjoy it. Leon, the captain, is his friend, and as they hadn't seen each other for some time they were delighted at being able to spend a few days together.'

'Are you saying that Leon went everywhere with you?'

'Of course not, but we were with him for meals, and in the night club – his wife was there, too.'

'My, you have been living it up!' Hilary's laugh held no mirth. 'Hob-nobbing with the captain and his wife. No wonder you come back starry-eyed!'

The sneer was plain this time; Hilary made no effort to hide it, and she gave a laugh of mocking amusement now which brought the colour rising to Marika's face. As always when she found herself alone with Hilary, she searched for an excuse to escape. Finding none, she leant back in her chair with a small sigh of resignation. Perhaps Nickolas would not be long; she hoped he'd just drop Souphoula at the cottage and come away, but thought it more likely that he would remain for a while discussing his father's changed condition.

Suddenly aware that Hilary's narrowed gaze was fixed on her watch, Marika's colour deepened, and she began to finger the watch with a little nervous gesture, waiting for Hilary's comment. Nickolas had bought it on the ship. He'd been so particular about getting her something 'really nice' that he had rejected every one the girl brought out. It wasn't until she produced this one – the most expensive watch in the shop – that Marika herself had been consulted. He asked if she liked it. She did, of course, but felt troubled over the price. Waving her timid objection aside Nickolas paid for it there and then and, taking her out on deck, put it on her wrist. Marika looked at it now. Small and dainty, with a delicate ribbon band of gold, it was the sort of present a man buys for the woman he loves.

No wonder Hilary stared in surprise, knowing as she did that their engagement was all a sham!

'Did ... Nick buy you that?' The words seemed to choke her, and the hand resting on the arm of the chair trembled slightly.

'Yes—' For some reason Marika felt guilty; the other girl was clearly hurt, and again Marika began to wonder what sort of a relationship had existed between her and Nickolas. 'He realized I hadn't one, and – and bought me this.' Although she ended on a note of apology Hilary's expression changed; she stared at Marika with open hostility, but any retort she intended to make was left unsaid. At that moment the door opened, and Nickolas walked in, bringing a sigh of relief from Marika. The tension in the atmosphere could not possibly escape him, and Marika watched his expression without quite knowing what to expect. To her astonishment his eyes became wary as, flicking from one to the other, they finally came to rest on Marika's flushed face.

'Come,' he said smoothly, 'we'll sit with Father for a while before dinner.' And without another glance at Hilary he opened the door for Marika to pass through before him.

'What were you and Hilary talking about?' he asked, apparently without much interest.

'It was — that is — Hilary remarked on my watch.'

He looked down at it, frowning strangely. Then his face cleared, and when they entered the bedroom a few moments later, his arm rested tenderly across her shoulders.

Everyone seemed unusually quiet at dinner that evening. Hilary was clearly in a state of suppressed anger; Nickolas appeared to be sorting something out in his mind with precise care, and Pitsa, never very talkative, seemed also to be occupied with her own thoughts. When the meal was over Marika and Nickolas went as always to Stephanos's room, but the old man had scant interest in their presence and Nickolas insisted on his settling down for the night. After making him comfortable, they left him and returned to the sitting-room. Hilary and Pitsa had books on their laps; Pitsa was reading, but Hilary's gaze remained fixed. Still angry, concluded Marika, but bored, dreadfully bored, too.

'Can we go for a walk?' she turned to Nickolas, smiling. 'I'd like to go to the Sanctuary again.' In a vague, expectant sort of way she felt he would choose that sacred spot to tell her of his love.

'Not tonight, Marika. I have some work to do.' He avoided her glance of surprise, adding deliberately, 'In any case you must be tired. I suggest you have an early night.'

No suggestion, but an order — gentle but definite.

There was no reason why she should be tired. True, they had been on deck until two this morning, and then driven up from Piraeus after the ship docked at nine o'clock. They arrived in Delphi before tea and since then she had done nothing but sit around. But what really surprised Marika was the assertion that he had work to do. Maybe he had, but it couldn't be that urgent, for he had been willing to remain with his father all the evening as usual.

For a moment she considered arguing – or rather, per-suading, but on noticing the inflexible lines of his mouth, she refrained.

'Very well, Nickolas,' she said flatly. Her 'good night' embraced them all; only Pitsa replied, and Marika went out and upstairs, a strange little access of fear tugging at her heart.

Flinging wide the window, she stood gazing out over the familiar landscape. It all seemed shadowy tonight, and more solemn than ever. The rock faces of Parnassus merged indistinctly with the sky, and the deeply-incised valley of the Pleistus took on the aspect of a bottomless chasm, mysterious, destructive. But then the valley opened out on to the sacred plain of Amphissa, with its great expanse of olive groves. In the far distance shone the Gulf of Corinth, and the little Bay of Itea with its curve of twinkling lights.

Marika felt she would never tire of the scene, for with every change of time, in every shade of light, its grandeur and its impression changed, too. One moment, the sense of divine closeness, of being drawn into the holy realm of the gods and ancient cults; the next, the illusion of drifting through space, or being anchored in a void of timelessness.

Startled into reality, she became aware of voices in the garden below. Nickolas and Hilary. . . .

Instinctively, she made to step back, into the darkened room, but her legs became suddenly weak.

'—dear Hilary, please don't fuss!'

'But the girl's in love with you!'

'Can I help that?'

Both spoke in whispers, but in the exceptional clarity of the air every word was audible to Marika, standing there in the silence of her room.

'You must have flirted with her, Nick. You might as well admit it!' He did not admit it, neither did he deny it. 'Are you quite sure your own heart wasn't affected, in the process!'

'Don't be ridiculous!'

A terrible pain throbbed in Marika's head. She thought nothing could wound more than that scornful exclamation, but she hadn't yet heard all.

'Then why did you buy her that watch?'

'It was a compensation present—' His voice dropped so low that Marika had difficulty in hearing his next words. 'I am deeply grateful for what she has done for Father.'

Compensation present. ... The lovely watch she had accepted from him so happily, that she intended to cherish for ever because of the tenderness in his eyes as he fastened it about her wrist. And it hadn't been tenderness at all, but gratitude.

She glanced down, as if compelled by some invisible force. Tears blurred her vision, but she saw that they stood close together, under the trees, by a little rustic garden seat. Hilary's tones of relief floated up to her, like a soft purr in the silence.

'Is that all? I felt so jealous, Nick.'

'Then you were very silly, my dear.'

'Perhaps, but you have never said you love me, never actually *said* it.'

'Are words necessary between you and me?'

A soft laugh answered him; Marika's lips quivered uncontrollably as she moved away, her tortured mind seeing them now in each other's arms. Quietly she closed the curtains, but not the window, lest they should guess she had heard.

Even in her misery she could not blame Nickolas. It was not his fault she'd mistaken gratitude for love. Her own stupidity overwhelmed her; how could she have ever imagined anyone like Nickolas would fall in love with her?

He was grateful ... and he pitied her. She recalled the sadness, the regret in his voice when he had told her it was dangerous to love too much— No wonder that terrible fear had flooded over her; it must have been instinct. Well, she didn't want his pity; he would soon realize she didn't need it because he'd never see her love again. When David had hurt her she had managed to laugh, and appear lighthearted – to hide her pain. She could do that again. . . .

That other had been a mere scratch, this was a wound, deep and enduring.

As was to be expected, sleep eluded her, and the following morning, Sunday, she came downstairs looking not only tired in body, but mentally fatigued. Nickolas, alone at the breakfast table, glanced up, and his smile immediately changed to an expression of deepest anxiety.

'What is it, child? Are you ill?'

Marika sat down, clenching her hands to stop their trembling. No doubt at all about his concern, but she wished he hadn't commented on her appearance; it only proved the difficulty of concealing her unhappiness.

'I didn't sleep very well.' She smiled at him and helped herself to rolls and jam. The food would probably choke her, but she intended to eat it, because if she didn't she was quite sure he would want to know why. And if he continued to show this anxiety she would burst into tears and tell him everything. That would embarrass him to such a degree that their relationship would become almost unbearable.

'You don't look as if you've slept at all,' he observed, examining her face closely. 'Perhaps I should have taken you out, after all.'

'But you had – work to attend to.' Marika made to fill her coffee cup, but he did it for her.

'What I had to do could have waited a while,' he returned, frowning. 'We will go for a walk this morning, and after lunch you shall go up and have a siesta.'

'I promised to go and see Souphoula today.' The coolness in her voice did not escape him; his brow contracted in puzzlement.

'We shall both go then – before lunch. I am determined you shall rest this afternoon.' The quiet emphasis, the implication that he would brook no argument, would have thrilled her a few hours ago; but she felt a hurtful lump in her throat and could not, after all, finish her breakfast.

Souphoula wanted to know all about their holiday, and Marika, contriving to hide her unhappiness, managed to put some enthusiasm into the account, though she did wonder if anything could be successfully hidden from those mysterious, watchful eyes. Nickolas, who had been strangely quiet during the short walk to Souphoula's cottage, seemed in some odd way relieved as he listened to her talking, and occasionally laughing at some incident that had amused her at the time.

But she never mentioned staying out on deck until two in the morning and, strangely, she made no reference to the little café at Patmos, either.

After leaving the cottage Nickolas insisted on taking her for a short walk as there was still an hour to go before lunch. They took the path into the hills beyond the Kastalian Spring, into the magic of the eagle-haunted crags of Parnassus. They spoke little. Marika was no longer thrilled by the spectacular beauty of the landscape; Nickolas, though putting her silence down to the fact that she hadn't slept, was again becoming puzzled.

'We must make the trip to the summit one day,' he said, hoping to arouse some response in her. 'It takes two days and one night, and we shall have to take everything with us, as there's neither food nor water to be had on top.'

She turned then, to look up at him, her eyes very dark and wide. For she knew after August the path to the summit of Parnassus could be obliterated by snow ... and she also knew that he would not leave his father now for two days and a night, at least, not unless it was absolutely necessary.

As it happened, it did become necessary for Nickolas to be away from home for a few days. He was needed at the hotel in Corfu, as the manager was again taken ill. Having consulted the doctor, who assured him that there was no immediate danger to his father Nickolas asked Marika if she would like to accompany him.

'I shall be busy, of course, and Corfu is not one of the most attractive of the Greek islands, but I'm sure you will enjoy it – and I shall try to take you out once or twice.'

'Thank you, Nickolas, but I don't want to leave Father again so soon.' Her lashes came down, hiding her expression. 'It is kind of you to ask me, though.'

'Marika, what is the matter with you!' Nickolas sounded as if his patience had been stretched almost beyond endurance, that he kept his temper only by the greatest effort.

'Nothing at all.' She looked up in feigned surprise, hoping her voice did not reveal that its lightness was forced. 'I don't know why you should ask.'

He glanced at her sharply, his eyes glinting.

'Don't you, Marika?' And then, persuasively, 'We'd be back in a couple of days; I think I can arrange a temporary replacement for Kinias, and if so, we shall be back by the day after tomorrow.'

Marika shook her head. Obviously he considered this a good opportunity to show her a little more of Greece – for hadn't he said it would be a shame for her to return to England without having seen something of his country? But she could not expose herself to more pain.

'I'll stay with Stephanos, if you don't mind.'

He stiffened visibly; he regarded her in frigid silence for a while and she was reminded of the old almost-forgotten arrogance before he said shortly,

'Very well, it's as you wish!'

David's letter arrived the day after Nickolas returned. Marika read it twice, then went out to see Nickolas in the office. He sat with sleeves rolled up, his back framed against the window, which opened on to a wide verandah. Trees, faintly stirring, gave welcome shade from the brilliant sun, and threw moving shadows across the desk, littered with papers and ledgers and glossy brochures.

'Can I come in, Nickolas?' She stood by the door, the letter in her hand, and spoke with forced gaiety. 'I'll not keep you a minute. It's about David.'

He had smiled on her entry, and his eyes flickered with a curious expectancy. Now they glinted coldly.

'Sit down, Marika.' As he leant back in his chair, a shadow caught his face; it became sinister, pitiless. Marika sat down, determined to retain her pose.

'He wants to come and see me. He's been working hard during the vacation and saved half the fare, so his parents have made up the rest.' Unconsciously, she waved the letter; the icy stare became more intense, but she managed to keep her eyes dancing with excitement. 'He cannot afford a hotel, so—' No mistaking his expression. She began to fold the letter and return it to its envelope.

'The fare can scarcely do him much good if he hasn't the money for accommodation.' His voice was quieter than expected and she glanced up again, hopefully.

'He— I wondered if he might stay here... ?' Her eyes pleaded, though his expression daunted her. The letter had come like an answer to a prayer, acted as a soothing balm to her injured pride, for David was so keen to see her that he had worked every day during the vacation in order to save the fare, or part of it. He now wished to spend the last two weeks with her in Delphi. 'I thought perhaps you would allow me to have a guest, Nickolas. He would be here for a fortnight.'

'Do you really want this – David to come here?' he asked, and Marika had the odd impression that, despite his frigid exterior, he was in some way hurt. . . . . What a stupid notion! She shook it off.

'Yes, Nickolas.' Marika allowed excitement to enter her eyes again. 'It would be lovely to have him. We used to be so happy together – and we'll have so much to tell each other!'

The familiar chirping of cicadas intruded into the long silence, and as Nickolas sat watching Marika the coldness gradually left his face. He astonished her by shaking his head in bewilderment before saying, in the same quiet tones,

'Is it so important to you, Marika, that you should see him again?'

For a moment she watched his hand resting idly on the desk, brown and strong. She had known its strength . . . and its tenderness. Her eyes misted over.

'It's terribly important – please let him come.' She looked at him imploringly, tears on her lashes. 'Please say yes, Nickolas, *please*!'

'Don't beg like that,' he returned angrily. 'There's no need!'

'Then he can come?'

'I'll think about it.'

'He asked me to let him know right away.'

There followed a long moment of consideration. It seemed to Marika that he had a sudden idea, and that whatever it was it tipped the scales in her favour.

'He can come on one condition,' Nickolas agreed at last. 'That is, that when you go about you take Pitsa and Kostos with you.'

She blinked at him.

'Kostos? Is he coming here?'

'He has a holiday due to him, and I have invited him to spend it with us. It wasn't to be until next month, when things become quieter, but I can bring it forward. Hilary can take over while he is here.'

Hilary. . . . He could send her away for a fortnight

without the least sign of regret? Marika knew why he wished to throw Kostos and Pitsa together, but she failed to make sense of his attitude regarding Hilary. Still, he was at liberty to go into Athens just whenever he wished, and Marika concluded he would be doing so quite often during the two weeks she was there.

She agreed to Nickolas's suggestion and was given permission to send the message to David. But she was also sternly reminded of her obligation to his father. He must not be neglected. Nickolas would expect her to go in as usual after dinner each evening, and also to read to him whenever he asked her to do so. On no account must Stephanos think that David was anything more than a friend.

Marika smiled bitterly as she left the office and went upstairs for the money to send the message. David was no more than a friend, never could be, but it gave her a strange satisfaction to know that Nickolas thought differently.

CHAPTER EIGHT

'Rik, you've changed!'

'In three months? – so have you, but never mind. Tell me all the news!'

To her surprise Marika had found herself looking forward with genuine eagerness to David's visit, and on his arrival she'd been actually excited. Perhaps it was because he represented home, and the sublimely uncomplicated past where life's only problems sprung from the shortage of money.

David had driven up from the airport by taxi, been introduced to Nickolas and his family, eaten his lunch, and now they were alone for the first time, sitting together on a hammock on a paved terrace under the welcome shade of the trees.

'Don't know where to begin. Lots of things have been happening and – oh, I've letters from your mum and the twins, but they're still in my case. Will they do later?'

She nodded.

'Start with the births. What did Mrs. Collins have?'

'A boy, Stephen.'

'She wanted a boy; is he nice?'

David laughed.

'New-borns look vile to me – yes, I suppose he is nice.' He paused. 'Now who's next? There's another Hardy annual – you knew it was coming, of course?' Marika nodded again. 'It's a girl, Norleen. Where do they get the names!'

'The boys will be disappointed,' grinned Marika. 'They hoped for a draw, but it's five-three.' She put her head on one side, counting mentally. 'That's right, they have eight now.'

'Now for the other news. Mr. Coombes has left the

post office, and we've got a funny old spinster who won't open the door once she's closed; she says if people can't remember what they want before closing time then they can do without.'

'How miserable! We've always gone to Mr. Coombes's side door.'

Taking a handkerchief from his pocket, David mopped his brow.

'This heat! Is it always so hot?'

'It was cooler when I first came. The spring's wonderful, David, and the flowers, they're heavenly!'

'I'll strip off in a few minutes.' He eyed her tan with envy. 'You look like a native. How far does it go?' he added, laughing.

Marika flushed and thought again how much he had changed since going to college.

'Would you like a cool drink?' she asked awkwardly, and again he laughed.

'I don't suppose you sunbathe in a dress. Have you a bikini?'

'I wear shorts and a sun-top.'

David's eyes roved admiringly.

'You've filled out; should look cute in a bikini. Why haven't you got one? Does he keep you short of cash?'

'Nickolas is most generous.' Frowning, she deliberately stressed the first word. 'I have more than enough.'

'Then why don't you buy one?' He eyed her curiously. There was a slight pause and then,

'I don't think Nickolas would approve.'

'What's it got to do with him? We'll buy one when we go to the shops,' he declared emphatically. 'Didn't think old Pluto would be such a stick-in-the-mud.'

Marika's frown deepened for a moment, and then cleared.

'Tell me about the spinney. Did they get planning permission?'

'No. Discovered the ground was liable to subsidence.'

'Good; we don't want any building there.'

'But we've a financier putting some of his thousands into the Gallimores' cottage. You knew it was sold?'

'It was up for sale, yes.'

'Three garages, patio, the lot. A few more like him moving in and bang goes our old-world charm for ever.'

'Happens everywhere,' put in Marika sadly, thinking of the lovely sixteenth-century cottage being transformed into a gleaming white villa. Her eyes wandered to the surrounding landscape. She saw it at dawn in all its wild majesty, and again when the encroaching dusk cast lengthy violet shadows, giving it a fairy-tale enchantment. She saw the great massif silhouetted against a sunset sky, or under a star-paved canopy when the twin peaks of the Phaedriades, bathed in a mist of silver, stood guard over the sun-god's hallowed domain. No one would ever build here. ... 'They do not build in Paradise,' she murmured, almost to herself.

'Is that how you think of it?' David scanned the scene appreciatively. 'You're right, too. This is a marvellous place. You're lucky, Rik, having all this for nothing.'

'I suppose I am.' Something in her voice made him glance at her curiously.

'Tell me about yourself. What has been happening to you?' He leant back in order to watch her changing expression in profile. 'You're not the same, Rik.'

Ignoring the last remark, she told him of her life here which was really one of strict routine. She talked of Stephanos, of Pitsa and Souphoula. She spoke little of Nickolas, and mentioned nothing about their recent holiday.

'We will go and see Souphoula tomorrow. She does not get out much – comes to see Father, of course, but has to wait until Nickolas can fetch her.'

'Father?' Again that curious glance. 'Why do you call him that? I heard you do so at lunch time.'

'He asked me to. He believes I shall marry Nickolas, as you already know.'

'And Souphoula. . . ? I heard you call her Grandmother.'

She shrugged.

'Just drifted into it, but mostly we call her Souphoula.' She paused reflectively. 'They're wonderful people, David. I love them all, Father, and Grandmother and Pitsa. . . .' Marika swallowed hard and a faint sadness entered her eyes.

'Hmm . . . the only one you don't seem to love is old Nick.' She frowned at that, but made no comment. 'I certainly don't blame you for that. He fits to perfection my idea of Hades himself.' He leant forward, laughing. 'Watch he doesn't drag you into the abyss!' He laughed more loudly and dropped a hand on to her knee.

Yes, people changed, she mused, rather sadly. A year ago David would never have made such a personal gesture. She was about to remove his hand when her attention became diverted. Nickolas, emerging from the office, stopped in his tracks as if unable to believe his eyes. For the merest second they rested on David's hand before moving to Marika's flushed countenance. His lips tightened and he went indoors.

'What's wrong with him?' David watched his retreating figure for a moment. 'Anyone would think you're really engaged!'

Although trembling slightly, Marika had to smile.

Had they been really engaged Nickolas would not have walked off like that!

Wiping his brow again, David announced his intention of changing, and got up from the hammock.

'I'll bring your letters down first, then you can be reading them.'

'You can find your room all right, can't you? – and don't use all the space, David. You're sharing it with Kostos; he'll be arriving in time for dinner.'

As she read her mother's letter Marika's heartbeats quickened, and when David came down again, clad only in shorts and sandals, she asked him about her mother's activities.

'Oh, yes; new fitted carpets, new furniture – goodness knows what they haven't got. Started buying just after you left. Caused quite a stir, as you can imagine, with everyone wondering how she was doing it, especially as Susan has thrown up her job again.'

'Susan out of work?' Marika blinked in puzzlement. 'Even with Susan working they can't afford all these things.'

'Getting a car next week; been ordered some time.'

Marika shook her head; she wondered why she trembled so.

'I can't understand it. Where *has* the money come from?'

'Stuff's all on the never-never,' he explained. 'Your mum eventually told mine.' He hesitated. 'You said in one of your letters that Nick increased your allowance.'

'That money was so that they could be more comfortable, not to encourage them to become further in debt.'

Again a hesitation. He felt reluctant to discuss such personal matters but her distress troubled him.

'Your mother confided in Mum that Mr. Loukas had paid off some debts as part of the bargain. Well, it seems that she expects he'll do the same again – at least, that's how Mum has sorted it out.'

'He won't, I know he won't – why should he?' Her heart actually thumped now, almost painfully against her ribs. In some inexplicable way she felt this would give Nickolas an added hold on her. Just how it would affect her she did not know, but there must be some reason for her sudden fears.

'I must write at once. These things must be sent back. Nickolas will not pay any more money; it isn't fair to ask him.'

David knew he'd have had to produce the letter some time, but he felt sorry he hadn't waited a while.

'Don't let it spoil our day, Rik. I'm sure everything will be all right. Your mother will probably be able to keep up the payments. Cheer up. I wish I hadn't given you the letter.'

'Do you really think she'll be able to pay, David? I don't know how much Nickolas sends. ...' Her eyes brightened. 'I'll write and tell her she can't have the car. Do you imagine it will be all right, then?'

He did not, but the pleading couldn't be ignored. In any case, he had no wish for the holiday to be spoiled by Marika's continued anxiety.

'I'm sure of it,' he replied, a lightness in his voice. 'Your mother was probably not serious. You know how women talk, and brag a little. I shouldn't expect she really means to ask for more money. Don't worry, Rik, Carol's working, so they're probably quite comfortably off.'

This calmed Marika, who decided to write to her mother at once. As David said, they would probably be able to pay for the other things so long as they did not have the car.

Hilary came out of the house a few minutes later, and after nodding to them, went into the office. Nickolas had ordered a taxi to take her into Athens and it was expected to arrive at two o'clock. Hilary's bag stood in the hall doorway, packed and ready. The office door closed behind Hilary; Marika wondered what they were doing, and at the same time thought it odd that Nickolas was not driving her into Athens himself. True, it was late to begin a return journey, but there had been nothing to prevent his starting out after breakfast. In any case, he could have stayed the night. ...

'I don't like that one.' David cut into her thoughts. 'Is she in love with Hades?'

'David, I wish you wouldn't call him these names!'

Anger made her voice rise. 'Please stop it!'

He stared, taken aback by the vehemence of her words. 'You're quite touchy about him, aren't you?'

Marika ignored that.

'Yes, she is in love with him,' she returned with some exasperation, looking along the drive as the taxi turned in at the gateway.

David pulled a wry face.

'The sort of bloke some women will fall for! Still,' he continued musingly as the taxi drew to a standstill and Nickolas and Hilary came from the office, 'I daresay he has all the finesse of experience, and that, I believe, is a most attractive asset in a man.'

Marika could find nothing to say to that, and they watched in silence as Hilary's suitcase was put in the car and Nickolas, after some final comment to the driver, closed the door. Hilary waved to him as the taxi reached the gate; Nickolas waved back and then returned to the office.

'She might be in love with him,' commented David in a strange tone, 'but is he in love with her?'

Swallowing the pain in her throat, Marika managed to say quite calmly,

'Yes. He's very much in love with her.' David's gaze became fixed upon her and she changed the subject, putting a forced lightness into her voice. 'You've told me all the news from home, now tell me about college.'

'College, or the girls?' he grinned.

'Both.' The girls didn't trouble her any more.

'Lots of work; first-year exams—'

'Oh, yes. How did you go on?'

'Passed. Don't ask me how – we all thought we'd fail.'

'Nonsense! You always worked hard. And look how you worked to get here. Was it at the garage?'

'No.' He shook his head grimly. 'On the new by-pass. Lord, was it tough! But the money was good, and when Mum and Dad promised to make up the fare if I earned half it was an added incentive. Then yesterday along comes Aunt Josie with thirty pounds for spending money.'

'Aunt Josie was always good to you. She enjoys giving and she only has her pension. I must buy her a present when we go out – probably in Athens.'

'Yes.' David grabbed her hand, his face eager, almost like a child waiting for a birthday to arrive. How young, thought Marika, and suddenly Nickolas appeared quite old. 'We must go places; you shall show me around!'

She explained about Stephanos, and about Pitsa and Kostos. David fell in with the suggestion readily.

'The more the merrier,' he said, and she smiled faintly.

No desire to be alone with her, no disappointment at their having company all the time. Marika felt overwhelmingly relieved by the knowledge.

They talked through the entire afternoon, taking their tea outside, and for a few hours they drifted back into the old relationship. But it did not take Marika long to realize that nothing had changed, that David had no affection for her whatever. Several times he had forgotten to be tactful, and she knew that he enjoyed himself immensely with the girls at college. At last she rose from the hammock and stood by the verandah, leaning against a slender support.

'Why did you come, David?' she asked quietly.

'Why do you think?' David held a glass of iced water to his lips and kept his eyes averted. 'To see you, of course.' Putting the glass down he went to her, taking her hand and curling his fingers round it in the way she had once found so pleasant. 'As I said in my letters, you're worth all the girls at college, Rik. But you're still a baby—' His grip tightened. 'I'll waken you before I leave.'

The faint smile reappeared. She was no longer a baby, as he called her, and as for the awakening. . . . He was too late.

'You wouldn't have spoken to me like that a year

ago,' she told him regretfully, and a frown creased his brow.

'You have to grow up, Rik. I was only a kid then. You should grow up; it's much more fun!'

Marika stirred restlessly, and pulled her hand from his.

'I have grown up – and I'm not so sure about its being more . . . fun.'

'I believe you have, too!' He stared wonderingly. She seemed taller, standing there by the post, one brown arm encircling it, and her hair gleaming against its vivid whiteness. He saw a new beauty in her face, a beauty enhanced by sadness and a strange sort of yearning. Her eyes were wide and dreamy, as if searching for some elusive haven that drifted out of reach.

He glanced back towards the office and his eyes became perceptive.

'Why have you come?' asked Marika again, bringing her gaze to his. 'Don't prevaricate, David. The truth can't hurt me.'

'No, I realize that.' For a while he hesitated, a flush of guilt upon his cheeks. 'I couldn't miss the opportunity of a cheap holiday,' he admitted baldly. 'All I had to find was half the fare. You know I always wanted to travel; well, this seemed a good chance to start . . . I'm sorry I used you, Rik. . . .'

Her gaze remained with him; she rested her cheek against the support, feeling its intense heat and the roughness of flaking paint.

'You haven't used me. It's Nickolas you've used.'

'He can afford it.' His voice sounded sulky, she thought and once more realized how young he was. 'Are you mad with me, Rik?'

A slight shake of her head answered him. Strangely, she neither blamed nor condemned him. There were others who would have done the same, she felt sure.

'I could ask why *you* let *me* come,' David commented in a sudden attempt to lessen his guilt. 'I once said you didn't love me. It was true then, but you didn't agree; do you agree now?'

For a moment she looked startled, then nodded her head.

'Yes, you were right,' she admitted. 'As for your first question, I don't really know why I wanted you to come. Perhaps I felt I needed an ally; someone who would give me support—' She flung wide her hands. 'I don't know!'

'How did it come about? He's not the type I'd expect you to fall for.'

Marika evinced no surprise, but she wondered how he had guessed.

'Does it show in my face?'

'I think you're managing to hide it,' was the comforting reply. 'You revealed it in other ways, though. Hating my calling him names, for one thing.' He paused in thought. 'Are you sure he's in love with Hilary?'

'I heard him tell her so – at least, when she asked him if he loved her he said words were unnecessary between them.'

David shrugged, and then,

'You little idiot, Rik! Why did you let yourself?'

'Can one prevent it? It just happened.'

'Sit down and tell me all about it.' Taking her hand, he led her back to the hammock. 'As long as we now understand one another we can speak plainly. It does you good to open up. Did you know how he felt about Hilary before you let yourself in for all this misery?'

'He seemed to have some sort of feeling for her,' she owned, sitting down again. 'But it really happened when we went on holiday. . . .'

When she had finished speaking David's forehead was creased in a frown.

'I don't like the fellow, but he doesn't strike me as the type who would deliberately flirt with a kid – an older woman, yes; I don't think he'd give a damn for her feelings because he'd expect her to know all the rules . . . but you. Did he actually admit to flirting with you?'

Marika wrinkled her brow, trying to recall what had been said between Nickolas and Hilary that night in the garden.

'She accused him of – flirting with me, and he didn't deny it, but I don't think he admitted it, either.' She stared at the open door of the office, a brooding expression on her face. 'It didn't seem to me like – like flirting. He was just kind, and sort of – gentle.'

'Did he kiss you?'

Her lips trembled.

'I thought it was because he loved me.'

'You don't know much, do you? I've kissed dozens of girls, but I don't love them— I'm sorry, Rik!'

'It's all right.' She managed to smile. 'This is spoiling things for us. I'll get over it in time.'

'Nothing so sure. I know exactly how you feel; been through it several times lately. Felt like throwing myself in the river, but it passes in a couple of weeks.' He paused. 'With you, Rik, it's your pride that's hurt, too. You talked just now of support. What do you want me to do?'

'I can't imagine what I expected you to do,' she replied vaguely. 'I just felt it would restore my self-respect if Nickolas could be made to think someone . . . cared.'

'It would restore your self-respect a jolly sight quicker if he could be made to think *you* cared – for someone else.' Marika said nothing, but stared at him wonderingly, and he went on, 'Are you sure you hadn't that in mind? Use me, Rik, by all means; it will ease my conscience – yes, honestly, I did feel some sense of guilt at using *you*. But now you can use me I feel much better about it.' He took her hand, curling his fingers round it in the old familiar way. 'That's what you want, isn't it? – to make him believe he's made one big mistake; that you don't love him at all?'

'That's what I want. Yes, David, you're right.' To

have her pride fully restored, to disillusion Nickolas completely; yes, she knew now that David had pointed it out that her one desire was to hold up her head again, to convey to Nickolas that his pity was wasted because she had no need of it.

'We'll have to indulge in a little flirting ourselves, just for effect. Do you mind?' He grinned at her, but she saw with relief that his eyes were serious.

'I don't mind what I do so long as I can convince him he's made a mistake.'

Dinner was a lively meal that evening. David and Kostos took to each other from the start and they talked and laughed a lot. Even Pitsa smiled more, seeming happier than she'd been for a long time. She wore a bright blue dress instead of her usual black or grey, and had a matching ribbon in her hair and a touch of rouge on her cheeks. She's pretty, thought Marika, and wondered if Kostos would notice it, too. Looking from one to the other, she could not help feeling that Nickolas was right. If the marriage had to be arranged, then Pitsa and Kostos were most admirably suited.

Nickolas also looked from Pitsa to Kostos, and his eyes flickered with satisfaction.

After dinner Marika and Nickolas went as usual up to Stephanos's room. The others intended going into the village, to join in Delphi's night life.

'David wants to see the cafés, to drink *ouzo* and listen to *bouzouki*,' Kostos said. 'See you later.'

Nickolas's eyes were hard as they went upstairs, and for the most part remained that way, softening only when his father looked at him. This was not often, for Stephanos lay very still that evening, his eyes half-closed most of the time.

Watching Nickolas, Marika wished they could return to the relationship that existed before the holiday. Despite his scoldings, and even his occasional indifference, life had on the whole been pleasant. Now he had adopted this cold and distant attitude towards her, but as her own coolness was responsible, she could scarcely blame him. But it made her position more difficult than ever, and tonight she felt her nerves becoming tensed by the ordeal of having to sit and pretend that she and Nickolas were in love.

To her dismay the old man noticed the difference in her, and asked if she were tired. He seemed faintly perturbed and she hastened to say,

'No, Father, I'm not in the least tired.'

'I have Nickolas, my dear,' he went on, ignoring her reply, 'so you must not feel obliged to sit here entertaining an old man, not if you don't feel up to it.' He searched her face again and her heart fluttered. How precarious her position! Stephanos seemed to miss nothing. 'Are you sure you wouldn't prefer to go to bed?'

Looking swiftly at Nickolas, she saw the challenge. Her lashes came down, masking her expression.

'No, Father,' she replied with faint emphasis. 'I'd rather stay for a while.'

A sardonic smile touched her fiancé's mouth; he had dared her to seize the opportunity of escape, but although his glance threatened, she was left with the impression that he would not have inflicted such cruelty on her a second time.

'Then I must admit I'm glad.' The sunken face became more tranquil. 'Tell me about this friend of yours. How long have you known him?'

'We went to the same school, but he's more than a year older than I.'

'Seems a nice boy, and studious. Has he a girl-friend?'

Her eyes flickered as she caught Nickolas's glance.

'He has dozens, or so he maintains,' she laughed, and her fiancé's brows rose, as if he thought she lied. If he had already begun to suspect she was David's one and only girl-friend, so much to the good.

139

'You miss your friends, I am sure,' said Stephanos, 'and it must be pleasant for you to have this young visitor. I was away from my country once, and all the time I longed to be back. Don't you ever feel the same?'

'I adore Greece,' she responded, but although her eyes glowed she felt her nerves becoming tensed again. 'And I love your people.' Would he notice the evasion? Marika dared not look at Nickolas. For the first time she began to wonder how long this difficult position would last. Frowning guiltily at her thoughts, she watched Stephanos as, in an abstract sort of way, he smoothed away an imaginary crease in the bed-cover, his thin pale hand rather unsteady. What was he thinking?

'This boy's coming has not unsettled you?' he asked oddly, glancing up under his white brows. 'You do not feel you would be happier at home?'

Marika felt the colour drain from her cheeks. Why should he be talking like this? Once again she was reminded of Nickolas's warning, of the need for caution. The old man's face, dark against the pillow, remained tranquil, composed, and yet. . . .

She had never expected the deception to be easy, but with Nickolas ever there as a prop, she had managed tolerably well. He now withheld his support, deliberately, it seemed to Marika, as if intentionally making things difficult for her . . . punishing her for something.

Her eyes pleaded for help. Perhaps that softened him, or perhaps his father's comfort was, as always, his chief concern – whatever the reason, he came to her assistance without hesitation.

'What a thing to ask, Father! Marika loves me – and I love her. How could she be happier back in England!' Reaching across the bed, he took her hand in his, holding it firmly, yet with a strange gentleness that brought a quiver to her lips. And the tone of his voice when he said he loved her! Could all this be feigned? There flashed through her mind several incidents that had puzzled her: his exasperation at her coolness; his suggestion that they should climb to the summit of Parnassus – knowing it could not take place until the spring; his wish that she should accompany him to Corfu. She'd concluded it was merely to show her more of his country; now, she wasn't so sure.

The conversation she had overheard seemed to lose some of its importance; in a vague sort of way she felt there could be some explanation for it. Dare she ask him about it? Becoming aware of the movement of his thumb across the back of her hand, she glanced up to surprise an expression she had seen only when on the ship. And suddenly all her love was released, freed from the restraint of the past few days. Her eyes shone as she tightened her grip on his hand. He appeared to be startled, and especially so when she said, in a voice of tender emotion,

'Nickolas is right, Father, I couldn't be happy anywhere without him now.' And she added, with a shaky, self-conscious little laugh, 'My heart's in Greece, so I really have to stay.'

Some time later they made Stephanos comfortable for the night, then left him. Outside the room, with the door closed, Marika said timidly,

'Nickolas, may I talk to you?'

'Yes,' was his grim reply. 'I think it is time you and I had a talk, Marika.'

As they reached the bottom of the stairs David came breezing in from the garden.

'Rik, there you are, sweetheart!' he exclaimed, after an instant's hesitation. 'Duty finished? Then come on out, darling, there's a wonderful moon – just the night for lovers!' He grabbed her hand with a quick, possessive gesture. 'You don't mind, Mr. Loukas? We've had a long separation, so there's a lot to make up!'

Nickolas's dark eyes swept over him arrogantly.

'Why should I mind?' And, with a glance of contempt at Marika, 'Before you go I must congratulate you on your acting; it was superb.' A slight pause followed before he added, slowly, deliberately, 'I hope mine was as convincing.'

For the next ten days Marika saw Nickolas only at meal times and during the hour or so which they spent each evening with Stephanos. For the rest of the time Nickolas appeared to be busy in the office, and to Marika's surprise he did not once go into Athens. Every other day he fetched Souphoula and took her back later. Sometimes he would sit alone in the garden, in the fresh, cool night air, or take a short stroll before going to bed. The idea of his being unhappy was absurd, yet it lingered in her mind. One night, unable to sleep, she had opened the window and stood looking out across the plain to the lights of the bay. Then she saw Nickolas, on the verandah, standing erect, so tall and straight and seeming to be deep in thought. How like a god he looked! Remote, unapproachable, and yet, in spite of this impression she ached to go to him, but the next moment desolation flooded over her in the knowledge that he did not wish for her company, and never would do so.

For the two couples it had been a busy ten days of sightseeing, for as Kostos had his car, they had managed to get about with ease. They'd explored the wild country in and around Delphi, and then ventured further afield. They visited Levadia, sauntering under the trees, had lunch in a little café where they ate small portions of lamb on skewers and drank Turkish coffee. David grimaced; Marika told him it was an acquired taste but most refreshing once you were used to it. She herself had hated it at first, for it was thick, and very sweet, but now she drank it like a native.

'I'll drink water,' David said, after another attempt to acquire the taste. 'It's more like syrup than coffee.'

They spent half a day in Aráchova, the charming Parnassan village, where Kostos took them to visit some friends of his. Later they strolled among the tourist shops and David bought some presents for his mother and his sister. Marika bought a hand-made rug for herself and another to send home, for David agreed to take it.

On another occasion they made the fourteen-mile journey to Amphissa. Kostos, an expert driver, negotiated the numerous hairpin bends with a skill that brought gasps of admiration from David, and caused Pitsa to look at him with an altogether new kind of interest.

The road to Amphissa traversed the olive country, with its welcome shade and charming admixture of colours – soft grey and green and silver.

They stopped at the lovely little village of Khrison, watching the men bringing their donkeys down to the well. The women came to fill their pitchers, then carried them away on their heads.

'Do the women really do all the work?' David wanted to know, his eyes following one old woman struggling along under the burden.

'In the villages, yes,' said Pitsa unconcernedly. 'The men just sit around in the tavernas all day and gossip.'

'Well, it seems all wrong to me!' returned David, 'Those men ought to be ashamed of themselves!'

'Here the man is— Oh, always I cannot find the word – no, *sometimes* I cannot,' laughed Pitsa. 'Here the man is always superior – not like in your country, David.'

In Amphissa they visited the Frankish castle and church, and then went on to Itea.

The following day they went into Athens, but that proved to be exhausting, for Nickolas would not allow them to stay overnight. David managed to do a little shopping after the visit to the Acropolis, and among other things he bought Marika a thin gold bangle. It cost only five hundred drachmae, but it was very pretty.

She wore it in place of the watch.

As the Athens trip had been so gruelling, especially

for Kostos, they all decided to have a quiet day in the garden before planning any more excursions.

'Why do they mess about with those beads?' David, reclining on an air bed, clad only in shorts, had his eyes fixed on Kostos, who sat on the opposite side of the terrace, his chair very close to Pitsa's.

'Worry beads? All the men have them. They're supposed to be a substitute for smoking.'

'They smoke as well.' David's eyes narrowed. 'That's an erotic movement.'

'Erotic?' Marika blinked at him.

'Didn't you know that the Greeks are the most amorous race in the world?'

'What about the Italians, and the French?' she retorted, defending the people she had come to love.

'No, the Greeks. It has recently been discovered.' He grinned up at her. 'You wouldn't do at all for old Nick, you know.' He stopped, contrite, as he saw her expression. 'Sorry; just trying to make you snap out of it.' He changed the subject. 'Did you know Kostos once had a crush on Hilary?'

Her eyes opened wide.

'No. Did he tell you?' Marika slid off the hammock and took possession of the air bed lying close to David's. 'He's much too young for her.'

'He knows that now.' David glanced across at the other couple. Marika followed his gaze. Kostos had his head close to Pitsa's cheek; he seemed to be saying something she liked to hear, for she smiled, then blushed enchantingly. 'Kostos and I have become quite good friends; perhaps you've noticed? Well, last night he was in a confiding mood – in fact, we were still talking at three this morning. Apparently when Nick installed him as manager at the Athens hotel Hilary was there, in charge, had been for a couple of months while Nick was finding a suitable replacement for the chap who'd left. She stayed on to show him the routine. The affair was progressing

144

nicely until old Nick gets wind of it – then off he takes Hilary and starts courting her himself!'

'You mean ... that Nickolas only decided he wanted Hilary after—? I don't believe it! That sort of dog-in-the-manger attitude would be totally foreign to his nature!'

'That wasn't the reason. Hilary owns half the business.'

'She has her husband's share?' So that was why she took such an interest in the business.

'Correct. So Nick decides to keep the money in the family. She dropped Kostos immediately she found that Nick wanted her. Went for the bigger prize, of course. Nick brought her away from the hotel, and they worked all day in the office here. I leave the rest to your imagination.'

Worked all day in the office. Somehow Stephanos must have got to know; that was how his fears had originated.

She shook her head in bewilderment.

'I can't imagine Nickolas marrying for money.'

'I must admit I can't, either. But much less can I imagine his tolerating another man interfering in the business. Besides, from what you heard, he's now in love with her, so can have his cake and eat it, so to speak.'

Yes, she mused, the whole arrangement appeared to be satisfactory from every angle. Then another thought occurred to her.

'What does Kostos think about our engagement? He doesn't know it's a sham.'

'Surprised him, naturally, but his attitude now seems to be one of satisfaction, as he believes she's lost both of them. Says it serves her right. And he's now overwhelmingly grateful to Nickolas, for what he terms his "escape", though he admits to feeling very bitter at first.'

Marika brooded on what she had heard. Kostos would, of course, soon know that his first assumption was correct. She felt bitterly disappointed in Nickolas for, although he now loved Hilary, his original reason for wishing to marry her had been entirely mercenary.

A merry little laugh rang out, breaking into her thoughts and she glanced swiftly across to the terrace where Kostos and Pitsa sat.

'Did Kostos say anything about him and Pitsa?' she asked curiously.

'Thinks she's marvellous – but surely you've noticed. It's because of Pitsa that he's so grateful to Nick for breaking up his romance with Hilary. His only concern is that Nick won't give his consent. In fact, he can't even pluck up enough courage to ask, he's so scared that he won't be accepted as her husband.'

'He wants to marry her? – oh, I'm so happy for her; she couldn't have anyone nicer than Kostos, and as for Nickolas's consent—' She had to laugh to herself over that. But the laugh died in her throat. Nickolas stood glaring down at her, lying – she suddenly realized – much too close to David because she had feared they might be overheard.

'Father is ready for you to read to him,' he said icily. 'Perhaps you will be good enough to put some clothes on and go to him.'

'Yes.' She got swiftly to her feet, reaching for a wrap. After putting it round her she went into the house, wishing she hadn't let David persuade her to buy the bikini— Why should she care what Nickolas thought of her? she asked herself, with an impatient toss of her head.

Nevertheless, when she returned to the garden some time later, she wore her shorts and a sleeveless blouse.

The following day Nickolas asked Kostos if he would like to stay on for another week.

'Yes,' he said, his eager glance straying to Pitsa, whose own eyes began to glow. 'But—'

'Then that's settled.' Nickolas turned to David. 'How about you – would you care to stay a little while longer?'

Marika's eyes became perceptive. Kostos still hadn't gathered the courage to speak to Nickolas about Pitsa, so he was being given more time. What puzzled her was her fiancé's unconcern at being away from Hilary for so long.

'Very much,' David was saying. 'College doesn't open until the middle of September – but I can't take advantage of your hospitality any longer.' He sounded quite genuine, thought Marika. Greece had done something to him; he'd become more serious, more mature. Nevertheless it was clear from his expression that he hoped Nickolas would press him.

'We shall be pleased to have you,' was all he said, but, despite the sardonic smile, Marika felt his dislike of David was not so great as his manner would imply.

A few days later Pitsa came to Marika in her bedroom, her face positively shining with happiness, and Marika wondered why she had ever thought the Greek girl lacked personality.

'You'll never guess, Marika, never!'

'Won't I?' Marika had to laugh. 'It's written all over your face!'

Pitsa blushed, then moved her head to bring it before the mirror, tidying a stray lock of hair. So unlike Pitsa – who hadn't seemed to care at all about her appearance. Marika's glance became affectionate; she hoped Pitsa would stay that way, for the majority of Greek girls appeared to neglect their looks after marriage. She had already learned that to a Greek woman marriage was the supreme objective; once having attained it, she seemed to give herself up entirely to the tasks of looking after her husband and bringing up a family.

'Kostos wants to marry me, and Nickolas has given his consent. I'm so happy, Marika – so very much I am happy!' She sat down on the bed. 'Who would have thought Kostos would want to marry *me*?'

'Kostos is a very lucky man,' returned Marika, and

Pitsa's blush deepened. 'Will Nickolas allow you to be alone now?' she added curiously.

'Not now – more than ever,' Pitsa said with a grimace, and then, her eyes twinkling, 'David and Kostos have arranged for us to go off on our own tomorrow. We shall all drive to Naupactus, as we said, but then you and David will bathe while we go off in the car for a little while. You do not mind?' she added in sudden doubt. 'In your country it is nothing for an engaged girl to be alone with another man?'

'No,' replied Marika with a tiny sigh. 'There would be no harm in it at all.'

Pitsa regarded her strangely.

'I think Nickolas must be adapting himself to your ways, for at one time he would not have let you go about with David like this. I would expect him to be very jealous and possessive.'

Marika could find nothing to say to this and she changed the subject, but a moment later Pitsa was saying, regretfully,

'I have been very stupid and obstinate. I see now that Nickolas must have been so anxious that Adolphos and I would steal ourselves.'

'Steal yourselves?'

'If a boy and girl fall in love against the wishes of their parents, they sometimes run away together. We say they have stolen themselves, and it brings dreadful disgrace on their families. But Nickolas need not have been afraid; I would never do that to *my* family.'

When Pitsa had gone Marika watched from the window; saw her join Kostos in the garden blow. Pitsa had not cared for Adolphos in a way that mattered and again Marika appreciated Nickolas's wisdom in putting a stop to the affair. Allowed her own way, Pitsa must surely have spoiled her life. Marika turned into the room. Everything had come out so right for Pitsa and Kostos . . . and for Nickolas and Hilary.

CHAPTER NINE

IT was arranged that Kostos should take David to the airport before returning to the hotel. They were to start out immediately after lunch, so they spent the morning wandering round the village, ending up in the museum. Marika had been several times, but David only once. Marika was content to stand admiring the bronze statue of the Charioteer while the others took David off to show him more of the treasures. But within a few minutes he had joined her again.

'Let them be alone for a while,' he said. 'I can't understand Nickolas; I'd have thought he'd be more enlightened. I don't believe they'd even kissed one another until we went to Naupactus.'

'In the remote villages couples are never alone for a moment until after the wedding,' she told him. And added, 'Then they're locked in the house together for three days and nights.'

'That sounds rather attractive,' he grinned, but at once became serious. 'Is that right – they're never left alone? I fail to see how they manage to fall in love under such conditions.'

Marika wondered if they did fall in love, and it struck her that Pitsa and Kostos were probably much more fortunate than the majority of couples.

They turned their attention to the statue, acclaimed to be the most perfect piece of sculpture in existence, and after staring at it for a long while David said, in a rather awed voice,

'I didn't realize it the first time I saw it, but it's marvellous! Gosh, Rik, you are lucky to be able to come in here just whenever the fancy takes you!'

'I know. I often pay my fifty drachmae just to stand

here and admire it.' She glanced around; saw the attendant. 'He's watching me,' she laughed. 'He knows I can't resist touching it.'

After a while the others returned, and when Kostos heard the conversation he said it was a pity David had not been able to see the Hermes for, in a different way, it was just as incredibly beautiful as the Charioteer. David at once bemoaned the fact that he'd been unable to visit Olympia, where the Hermes was the most famous exhibit in the museum.

'You'll be coming back, though, often,' asserted Kostos, 'and you must spend some time with Pitsa and me. It's easier to get about from Athens. I promise we'll take you to Olympia the next time you come. After Delphi you may be rather disappointed in the site, though. There is no setting in all Greece as dramatic as the one here.'

Leaving the Charioteer at last, they went again to view the magnificent friezes and pediments from the various treasures that had existed on the site of the Sanctuary. Pitsa, her shyness gone, answered all David's questions, and as Marika watched him she thought again how mature, how serious he had become. They were standing before the famous winged Naxian Sphinx; David, watching Pitsa intently, seemed avid for information. It was the Sphinx, she was saying in that sweet, husky voice, who sat on the wall of Thebes, challenging all who wished to enter the city to solve the riddle: 'Four foot, two foot, three foot'. Only Oedipus solved it.

'Man it was,' Pitsa smiled. 'A baby walks on four feet, a young man on two, and an old person with the aid of a stick.'

But solving the puzzle helped in Oedipus' downfall for, after entering the city of Thebes, he married Jocasta, his own mother. Pitsa went on to relate a little of the king's tragic life, during the whole of which he was mercilessly pursued by the gods. He found peace at last only in death on the sacred hill of Colonos.

David regarded Pitsa in a new light, bringing a deep flush of pleasure to her cheeks. Kostos took her arm and led her firmly away to look at something else.

David grimaced.

'Jealous,' he laughed.

'Pitsa will be delighted. I'm so thrilled for her, David. She doesn't appear to have had much pleasure in her life until now.'

He stared after her.

'You know, Rik, I wouldn't mind a Greek girl myself.'

'You're incorrigible!' she laughed as they, too, moved on to another room.

On the way out they stopped at the top of the stairs to admire the Navel of the Earth, the Omphalos, which had been removed from Apollo's temple.

'This is not the original,' explained Pitsa. 'The Romans made it, but it's an exact copy. Apollo, the god of wisdom, sat on the Omphalos to announce his advice to the suppliants – through the Oracle, of course.'

'God of wisdom?' David looked puzzled. 'I thought he was the god of light, of the sun?'

'Of wisdom, too. He gave us that famous maxim, "Know thyself"; it was written above his temple.'

On their way back the two girls nodded and smiled several times to the villagers, and Pitsa spoke in Greek to a man sitting astride a mule. His wife trudged behind him, hot and tired. David frowned heavily but said nothing until, a few moments later, he noticed a woman tending goats on a distant hillside. She wore the usual black garments and the sun blazed mercilessly down on her.

'The women here are no more than possessions! I hope, Kostos, you're not going to treat Pitsa like that!'

'A woman here is always subordinate to her husband,' he responded calmly. 'I do not think Pitsa would wish it to be otherwise. But that does not mean we treat our

151

women callously, as you appear to think.'

'I don't know what else it is – the women doing all the work, and the men just sitting around doing nothing! You don't call it callous for a man to ride while his wife walks behind – obviously exhausted?'

Even Marika had to laugh at his indignation. She herself had become used to seeing the women working and the men idling, though at first she'd been just as appalled as David.

'Do not worry, my friend,' laughed Kostos. 'I love Pitsa and so shall work for her. We will be living in Athens, and there it is different. Do not scowl so, David!'

Pitsa turned to David, smiling placidly.

'The Greek husband is always the master,' she told him. 'For me, I expect it, but for Marika it will be difficult at first because in England you have the equality.'

David cast Marika a sideways glance; clearly he considered her fortunate not to be marrying Nickolas.

They arrived back at the house a little early for lunch, and after tidying herself Marika came down to find David alone in the sitting-room. He seemed serious – and much older than when he arrived.

'I shall never feel the same, Rik.' He made room for her on the couch. 'Everything you said in your letters was right. This place does something to you.'

'Yes,' she agreed, sitting down beside him, her eyes resting on the very beautiful ikon fixed above a shelf on which stood two primitive votive offerings, crude clay figures such as a child might model almost at its first attempt. They had come from a tomb in Cyprus and were over four thousand years old. 'Yes, it does something to you.'

'I shall spend less on the girls,' he stated emphatically. 'I'm going to save hard so that I can come back next year.'

Next year. . . .

'I shall be home by then,' and, without warning, the

tears rolled slowly down her cheeks. Producing a hand-kerchief, David began to dry her tears.

'Don't cry, Rik. You'll come back, too.'

Marika grabbed the handkerchief and rubbed her eyes hard.

'Do I look as if I've been crying?' she asked urgently, getting up to glance through the mirror. 'Yes, I do. I can't go in to lunch like this!'

'No, well— Can't you put some make-up on?' David looked vague.

They heard the muted sound of the gong. Marika rubbed hard again, shaking her head.

'We'll have to go. Nickolas hates you to be late for meals.'

Nickolas subjected her to an intense scrutiny, then gave her no further attention throughout the meal.

After lunch Marika and David went over to the office.

'I just want to thank you, Mr. Loukas.' David spoke with a sincerity that pleased Marika, as he went on to say what a wonderful holiday he had had. 'I do thank you,' he said again.

'That's all right; you have in fact done me a service.' Nickolas paused. 'As for Marika, she appears to have de-rived a considerable amount of enjoyment from your visit. Isn't that so?'

She did not reply immediately, for David had slipped an arm about her shoulders. She wished he hadn't, for it was no longer necessary. Nickolas had seen enough during the past three weeks to disillusion him completely. His attitude gave every indication that he now believed her to be in love with David.

'Yes, I have enjoyed David's visit,' assented Marika quietly, realizing that both men were awaiting an answer.

'Kostos tells me you are hoping to return next year?' Nickolas spoke in tones of cool courtesy which lacked any real interest.

'If I can save enough.' David looked rueful. 'It's difficult when you've only the vacations – and even then there may not be enough jobs to go round.'

Nickolas agreed about the difficulty, and they fell into casual conversation until Kostos, having been to fill up with petrol, came to say he was ready to go.

Marika viewed the departing car with a mixture of relief and regret. She went up and read to Stephanos, who seemed strangely quiet, and no matter how Marika tried, she could not quell the misgivings which persisted throughout the afternoon.

The sun was beginning to set when, feeling restless, and anxious about Stephanos, she left the house and walked slowly down the road towards Souphoula's cottage. The houses, precariously perched among the heights, were bathed in a golden radiance; the landscape became softer and yet more mysterious in that curious mixture of light and shadow falling on the sun's rapid descent.

A sense of depression marred her usual pleasure in the familiar scene. Her thoughts, uncontrolled, flitted from one thing to another; each added to her unhappiness.

How would Pitsa react to the broken engagement? Without doubt it would be a disappointment to her, for the two girls were now devoted friends. But she had Kostos and Marika hoped that would help her not to feel too unhappy. A deep sigh escaped Marika as, nearing the cottage, she visualized Souphoula sitting there, straight, grotesque almost, in her sombre black, her eyes watchful, all-penetrating. Yet how she had grown to love her! For there was nothing superficial about Souphoula; she was deep, and sincere.

Nickolas had certainly spoken the truth when he said it was dangerous to love too much. She'd left herself open to pain that would not heal for a very long time. And what of Greece ... so soft and warm? The country had claimed her, made her a part of it. The white house clinging to the hillside, the garden with lilies and oleanders and hibiscus, with shady plane trees and vine-draped arbours; the enchantment of shining mountains and eagle crags, of olive groves and the shrine so long abandoned. With all these she had lived intimately; she'd achieved a sense of belonging, and even begun to take the overwhelming hospitality and friendliness of the Greeks for granted.

To leave, without hope of ever returning, was almost more than she could bear.

Souphoula sat in the dimly-lit room, a waxen statue, erect and stiff. A mere flicker of her eyes expressed a welcome.

'Is Pitsa not with you?' she murmured as Marika sat down on the couch.

'She'll be along soon. I came on ahead.'

'Why?'

Marika plucked absently at a button of her blouse, her eyes very dark and uncertain.

'I don't know.' So difficult to explain the comfort she derived from these moments alone with Souphoula. 'I've been reading to Father. Souphoula, he's gravely ill.'

'Stephanos has been gravely ill for a long while, my child. We are all resigned.' Her eyes were devoid of expression. It was hard to estimate the extent of her sorrow. Did she suffer as deeply as Nickolas? Which was the more heartbreaking, for a mother to lose her son – or for a son to lose his father? Her own sense of loss would be great, she knew, and a sudden access of pain became reflected in her gaze.

Souphoula regarded her in silence for a long moment.

'Your young friend has gone?'

'Yes.' Marika nodded. David had said good-bye to Souphoula the previous evening. 'They went directly after lunch.'

'Is Hilary back?' A soft and curious inflection had entered the old woman's voice, which caused Marika to send her a sharp glance of puzzlement.

'She's expected to be back before dinner.'

'So Pitsa and Kostos are to be married. That should relieve Nickolas of some of his worries.'

Some ...? Marika frowned and stared at Souphoula in the semi-darkness wondering why, after inquiring about Hilary, she had so abruptly changed the subject. There was perception, yet at the same time obscurity in her manner. What lay behind those dark, inscrutable eyes?

Pitsa often spoke in awesome tones when referring to her grandmother's great wisdom. Souphoula, she maintained, knew everything that you felt or thought, everything that went on around her. The old woman's eyes still penetrated, though the rest of her face was a mask. Yes, Marika could believe that very little escaped her, and she felt no surprise at hearing her say,

'Do you wish to talk about it?' The voice was soft and faintly persuasive; Marika gave a little sigh and for a moment hesitated, not knowing how to answer. Souphoula added, 'You may have convinced Nick that you're in love with that boy, but you haven't convinced me.'

That did startle Marika, for, on her instructions, David had acted with supreme caution. Their intention had been to mislead Nickolas – and no one else.

'You will not tell Nickolas?' she said urgently.

'It's no business of mine; but I would like to know what went wrong. You were happy when you returned from your holiday.'

Happy. ... A bitter smile curved Marika's lips. Her happiness had merely been a prelude to this incurable ache of misery.

'I thought Nickolas loved me,' she submitted, 'but I should have known better.'

The black eyes flickered in puzzlement.

'He doesn't love you?'

Marika shook her head and went on to repeat what

she had overheard. Receiving this without any show of concern, Souphoula remarked drily,

'You didn't have to listen.'

'I couldn't help myself,' confessed Marika, the colour rising in her cheeks.

'Pity. There's rarely anything to be gained from eavesdropping.'

Marika couldn't agree. Far better to learn of Nickolas's feelings that way than to suffer the humiliation of revealing her love and then learning the truth.

'So your reaction was to convince him that you cared for David?' For the first time Marika saw a flicker of amusement in the old woman's expression. 'I suppose Nick believes you intend to marry the boy?'

'I hope so,' came the fervent response. Souphoula's lack of concern hurt deeply. Marika hadn't expected any outward display of sympathy, but she had expected to be aware of its presence.

'The young seem to revel in complicating their lives,' said Souphoula enigmatically. 'Age certainly has its compensations.' The amused expression lingered, increasing Marika's indignation – and yet there was something besides amusement in those piercing eyes as they searched her face narrowly before Souphoula added, in strangely gentle tones, 'I once told you not to worry too much about Hilary. . . . And I meant it.'

Marika stared blankly. What could Souphoula mean? Before she had time to ask for an explanation, Pitsa entered, and the subject had to be dropped.

With the familiar glow of happiness on her face Pitsa announced that the wedding would take place in October, and she and Kostos were to have Nickolas's apartment at the hotel. Marika turned in surprise.

'But won't he need it?'

'I don't suppose, when he is married, that he will wish to sleep away from his wife,' Pitsa laughed in a slightly teasing sort of way and, catching Souphoula's eyes,

Marika flushed hotly. 'Nickolas now conducts most of his business from here, which is much more convenient, for he used to get so dreadfully tired.'

After tea Pitsa asked Souphoula if she could show Marika her 'dowry' – or part of it.

'Certainly, child. Perhaps it would be better if you took your things home now.'

'It will be just as easy to move them from here,' Pitsa said, opening one of the large drawers and taking out some beautiful hand-woven blankets. The great chest stood along one wall of the room, and Marika had often wondered what the drawers contained. 'Nickolas says he will take them for me.' She drew out more blankets, embroidered sheets and pillow-cases, bed-covers and masses of underwear, all hand-made and wrapped in linen as a protection against dust and dirt.

'Where did you get it all?' gasped Marika. 'There's so much!'

'Mother did some, and my aunts. Souphoula has made most, though.' Pitsa sat on the floor and pulled out another drawer, equally crammed with bedding and covers.

'When a female child is born all her relations begin making things for her *prika*,' Souphoula explained.

'As soon as she is born?'

Souphoula nodded.

'She must also take to her husband land and money. But I presume Kostos will have extra money instead of land. It is seldom that a girl can find a husband unless she has this dowry – though in the towns people are becoming more enlightened. Kostos may not wish for anything at all,' she added, though with some doubt.

On the way home Pitsa talked excitedly about the wedding, saying that Kostos was coming for the weekend, when he and Nickolas would fix the exact date.

Hilary had arrived, and she and Nickolas were in the office when the two girls passed on their way through the garden. At dinner they talked all the time, mainly about business, but there was an underlying affection both in Nickolas's manner and his voice. Hilary later congratulated Pitsa on her engagement, but scarcely spoke to Marika, for her attention was mainly with Nickolas. She openly made play with her eyes until even Pitsa noticed and cast an anxious glance at her friend. But Marika kept her eyes lowered and, at the first opportunity, excused herself and went upstairs to Stephanos.

'You would m-marry me, knowing how I feel about ... David?' White to the lips, Marika faced Nickolas across his desk in the office. He, too, seemed pale beneath the tan, but his face held all the merciless arrogance of that first meeting, his voice that inexorable quality that had once before convinced her of the futility of argument.

'I am not interested in your feelings,' he returned icily, 'but I am concerned with my father's happiness. We shall be married just as soon as it can be arranged.'

'You can't make me. ...' To her own ears her voice lacked conviction. She remembered thinking that what this man wanted he would have, and a sudden desolation swept over her. And yet, dominating all other emotions, was the staggering knowledge that Nickolas's love for his father outweighed his love for Hilary. She tried to read his expression, to discover the extent of his sacrifice, but all she saw was a harsh, impassive countenance and a mouth set in a determined line. 'I won't marry you, Nickolas,' she said, with an effort to appear calm, but as his jaw tightened she added desperately, 'Mother would never give her consent.'

'Your mother already has—' He tapped a letter lying on the desk. 'At a price.'

'She wrote to you ...? You've paid her debts?' She stared at the letter for a long moment. It seemed to have a fascination for her. 'Mother doesn't even know whether or not I want to marry you!'

'I expect she took that for granted, otherwise I should hardly be asking for her consent.'

A faintly bitter smile curved her lips. Nickolas was an expert at the art of dissembling; she could imagine how easily her mother had been misled.

'We made a pact,' she reminded him quietly, 'and your paying my mother's debts cannot make any difference to it. I have fulfilled my part, and even if I've made a few minor slips that's nothing to do with our bargain. You can't now introduce new conditions to suit your own ends.' Again she contrived to appear calm as she stood before him, her hands resting on the desk. She had come a long way from the 'street urchin' that David had so often teasingly called her. Not only had she matured, but she'd acquired a special delicacy and grace, and a beauty, unpretentious, yet nevertheless very real.

'You are entirely responsible for what's happened. It was no minor slip, as you term it, that resulted in his guessing the truth.'

The sun sent a brilliant ray of light across the desk; Nickolas moved to draw the curtain and when he turned he remained close to her – too close for comfort.

'Why me? What have I done?' The desire to put some distance between them was almost irresistible, but she was suddenly reminded of what Souphoula had once said about his becoming dangerous only when his anger was suppressed.

And his anger was well under control at present.

'Don't you know what you have done?' He gripped her wrist; David's bangle cut into her flesh. 'This! In Greece a woman does not discard her fiancé's present – replace it with another man's gift! I warned you from the first that extreme caution was necessary. If you choose to flaunt my advice then you will take the consequences.'

'Father did not mention anything to me, at least. . . .' Marika put a trembling hand to her mouth. 'He asked me who bought it – yes, I remember now.' She looked up at Nickolas fearfully.

'And you told him.' He released her hand; she rubbed soothingly at the mark on her wrist. 'You actually told him that David had bought it for you.'

'I didn't stop to think,' she confessed, her voice barely audible. 'He didn't pursue it, though; he just let the matter drop and – and I thought no more about it.'

'He did; plenty. He asked me what was wrong that you preferred it to the watch I bought you, and he mentioned several blunders you had made at various times.' His eyes were narrowed and coldly accusing. 'You knew how precarious the position, knew he'd had suspicions on and off practically from the beginning, yet you take a risk like that. We've managed until now to allay his suspicions – and I believe we could have continued to do so had you kept up your . . . pretence of loving me. As it is, only positive action will suffice. We shall have to marry.'

The coolness of him! – as if he had no feeling at all for Hilary.

'Did Father actually say that he – he knew what we had done?' she managed to ask, after a long silence.

'Not in so many words,' and, as he saw a flicker of hope appear, 'Make no mistake; he is fully aware that he's been deceived.'

'Then he knows we are not – not in love with one another, so what good will it do for us to marry?'

Nickolas did not reply immediately. Moving over to the window, he stood with his back to it, arms folded, his whole attitude one of superiority; he seemed to assume the rather nonchalant air of the victor, as if her surrender was already complete. Marika felt the colour return to her face . . . angry colour.

'As you know,' he said in cool and even tones, 'Father's one concern is to keep Hilary and me apart. Being aware of my views on marriage he will be satisfied, once you and I are married, that there could never be any possibility of my marrying Hilary. No doubt he would have preferred a – love match, but he has a very great affection for you and he will be quite content to see us married.' He paused. 'One thing I wish to make clear. If I force this marriage on you—'

'You can't force it on me, Nickolas! We made a contract and I've kept to it—'

'You have not, otherwise we shouldn't be in this position.'

'You didn't stipulate that if I made a mistake I would have to marry you.'

'I warned you, more than once, that I would go to any lengths to ensure my father's happiness. As I was saying, if I force you into this, it will end there. Had it been that you married me willingly. ...' It seemed for a moment that all arrogance left him and that he spoke to himself, as if forgetting her presence. And Marika saw him again as she had seen him on the ship, with a great tenderness erasing every harsh line from his face, but even as the tears pricked her eyes and an ache of longing enveloped her she saw the arrogance return and the hard light come back into his gaze. 'I shall force nothing else on you, Marika, you need have no fear of that.'

She flushed, and her eyes became very dark. Could a man like Nickolas live a life like that? Or did he mean to keep his ...? Perhaps he'd have only one pillow friend – Hilary.

He hadn't actually said he would stop her mother's money if she refused to marry him, but she knew he was capable of doing so. On the other hand, she had done as he had originally asked and, despite the failure of his plan, she felt he might be lenient and continue the allowance. But, whatever his intention, she did not see why she should sacrifice her life, either for her mother, or for Stephanos. To live with a man she dearly loved and to know he neither cared for, nor wanted her, was something she was not willing to endure. He could not expect it, none of them could.

'I won't marry you,' she said again, though she trembled inwardly. 'I can't ruin my life, even for Father.' She wondered why that name came so easily to her lips under the present circumstances – and she wondered why, despite her resolve, she still felt afraid.

'Ruin your life?' he exclaimed so harshly that she took an involuntary step backwards. 'You're convinced that you and David are suited, but he is not right for you in any way at all!'

She made no comment. The pretence of loving David had proved a strain from the start, and it was no longer necessary to keep it up. Nickolas showed only complete indifference to her feelings. Looking up, she saw the inflexible set of his mouth, and that sinister, almost evil quality that contrasted with the otherwise clear contours of his face. Still acutely aware of the strength of his domination, she became filled with an urgent desire to make him realize he was human, to strip from him that god-like attribute of invincibility.

'I'll never marry you, never! You can't make me – and you know it. I'm going home, do you hear? – right away!'

'Going home?' Nickolas regarded her coolly, and she bit her lip in frustration. He would never give her the money for her fare, and she did not see how else she could obtain it.

'You can keep me here until it suits you to let me go,' she agreed in quieter, more controlled tones, 'but you can't force me to marry you, Nickolas.'

A dark flush rose under the tan; she sensed anger, frustration, and a deep unhappiness as he regarded her in silence for a moment before, turning abruptly, he left her standing there, angry with herself and everyone concerned for the sudden weight of guilt that oppressed her.

Hadn't she triumphed? — brought him crashing down from his lofty pedestal? This was the only time he had not had the last word, the only time he'd been taught that he couldn't dictate other people's lives. Why, then, this complete lack of satisfaction? Why this overwhelming sense of guilt? Marika put her face in her hands and wept — wept bitterly for no reason that she could define.

A little while later, feeling more composed, she left the office and walked slowly across the garden towards the drive. Souphoula would give her comfort— Marika stopped abruptly, putting a trembling hand to her mouth. How could she face her now? Did she know what had happened? Did those piercing black eyes reflect the same unhappiness that had appeared in those of her grandson a short time ago? With a sinking heart Marika retraced her steps and entered the house. Reaching the top of the stairs, she glanced along the landing to the door at the end and hesitated. Then, going to her own room, she took off the bangle and fastened Nickolas's watch on her wrist.

Stephanos lay very still, his eyes scarcely moving as Marika sat down on the bed. She had thought that Nickolas's unhappiness was great, but this surpassed anything she had ever known. She recalled his kindness, his generosity over the years, her father's affection for him. She thought of Souphoula, of Pitsa, and the only important thing was that these people whom she loved should not suffer by any action of hers. Of her own life and future she dared not think. Had Nickolas married her for love she knew he would have adapted himself in some measure to her own ideas, have treated her as an equal, extending to her the respect which she would naturally give to him. But how would he treat her now? Would she be regarded in the same light as the majority of wives in Greece — as a possession? She dwelt for a moment on the menial tasks of the bedroom, which even Pitsa expected to perform, when the wife took each garment from her husband as he undressed, and folded it neatly. The following morning she had to stand there, in an attitude of servility, and pass him his clothes one by one. These tasks she would of course be spared, but what of her everyday life? Unable to dwell on the possibility of long years of subjugation, she dismissed those terrifying thoughts and smiled down at Stephanos, praying that she might act naturally and with conviction.

'Has – Nickolas told you the news, Father?' She came straight to the point, fearing a delay would result in her courage failing her. 'We're to be married – just as soon as it can be arranged.'

The pale eyes flickered, then became fixed. It was a tremendous effort for her to meet that gaze without flinching, but somehow she managed it.

'Nickolas has been talking to you? What sort of a hold has he on you, child, that he forces you to do these things? Why did you come here in the first place?'

Marika's heart pounded; she had expected her task to be made easier by the fact that Stephanos had not actually admitted knowing of their deception. But now he had admitted it – and when she was alone with him. Never had she needed her fiancé's help more than now, but she could not see his coming again so soon after that uncomfortable visit of only an hour ago.

She could not lie, and she was no dissembler like Nickolas, so she told him the truth, omitting nothing except what she had overheard between Nickolas and Hilary that night when they were standing together in the garden. When she had finished she was amazed to see the relief on his face and a contented smile appear about his lips.

'It is gratifying to know of this abounding love my son has for me,' he sighed, making a feeble effort to sit up. Marika rose instantly, easing him on to the pillows and making him comfortable.

'Is that better?' She smiled at him tenderly and with

infinite compassion. 'Are you quite comfortable now?'

He nodded.

'You're sure, my daughter, that you really wish to marry Nick?'

'Quite sure, Father. I spoke the truth when I said he wasn't forcing me into it. In fact, he believes I shall not marry him, for I told him so a few minutes ago.'

'And you changed your mind because of me. . . .' Lapsing into thought, he remained silent for a while, and then he said a strange thing. 'If I were not absolutely sure that this marriage would turn out right I'd object to it, no matter what the cost to myself. But our men are faithful, Marika. You will have no fears about your husband; from the moment you say you will marry him he'll be finished for ever with Hilary.' He paused, again in thought. 'What makes you think Nick doesn't care for you? If this is true then he is an excellent actor.'

She had to smile, though rather wanly. No doubt about it whatsoever, Nickolas was an excellent actor!

'I'm quite certain he doesn't love me,' she said quietly. 'But please don't ask me how I know.'

His eyes were puzzled, but he respected her wish not to be questioned.

'You love him, though, and that will suffice. He cannot long remain insensitive to it.'

An inaudible sigh escaped her. How simple he made it sound! Still, if his deductions satisfied him, freed his mind from worry, nothing else mattered for the present.

'Does Souphoula know of your doubts?' she asked suddenly as the idea occurred to her.

'My mother is too old for these worries,' he replied. 'I did not intend to mention it.' His thin hand toyed absently with the beautiful embroidery of the bed-cover; he began to murmur to himself in weak, low tones and Marika had difficulty in understanding much of what he said. But she did gather that he intended to speak to Nickolas about Hilary's going away – though there seemed to be some difficulty regarding it. Then she realized that Hilary not only owned half the business, but also half the house. Nickolas had wished to buy her out immediately after Andreas's death, but she had refused to sell. Stephanos continued to mumble on, almost unaware of Marika's presence, for he often lapsed into Greek and she lost the trend altogether. Picking it up again, she heard him deploring the fact of his foolishness in dividing everything equally between his two sons, but how could he know what would happen? Then he frowned heavily, mentioning something about his presumption regarding Nickolas and Hilary, and that 'poor Nick might only have been holding the – the—' He went off into Greek then, obviously being unable to express himself in English, and she heard the word, *'diabolos'.*

He exhausted himself and, with a feeling of guilt, Marika insisted on his lying down and resting before Pitsa arrived with the tea.

'I've excited you, Father,' she murmured apologetically. 'Lie down – further down.'

He obeyed meekly – and she found herself wondering if he'd ever possessed the dynamic personality and vigour of his son.

He did not thank her for the decision she had made, but his smile of gratitude filled her with a strange contentment. His fears were dispelled for good; for the short time left to him he would know tranquillity and peace. And a certain serenity entered into Marika herself as she went downstairs to inform Nickolas of her decision. There was a special dignity about her, too, which caused Nickolas to stare at her in faint surprise as she stood just inside the door of the sitting-room, looking at him intently for a while without speaking.

Slowly she advanced into the room, and came close to him, sitting there on the couch, his newspaper lying folded on his lap.

'I've seen Stephanos,' she told him quietly. 'He's perfectly happy now.' Nickolas removed the paper from his lap and stood up; Marika smiled faintly. How like the Greek male! He would not allow her to look down at him.

'You will marry me?' he asked, on that oddly tremulous note which had so surprised her on their first meeting.

Her very nod seemed to reflect the new dignity that had come to her. It was a mere inclination of the head, yet firm and decisive; it brought a flicker of appreciation to her fiancé's eyes, and a faint smile to his lips. She misunderstood, taking it to be amusement tinged with triumph.

'I want you to understand,' she said coolly, 'that I am marrying you of my own free will. You have not forced me into marriage, Nickolas. You never could do so – please remember that.'

His smile deepened and this time it did hold some amusement.

'I will remember, my dear—' He paused to allow his next words to sink in. 'And I hope you will remember it, too.'

Marika blinked at him, for there appeared to be a hidden threat in those words. Her dignity deserted her for a moment, replaced by fear.

But the next moment Nickolas had taken her hands, holding them firmly, and the smile on his lips was almost tender as he said, with deep gratitude,

'Thank you, Marika. Thank you for making Father happy.'

CHAPTER TEN

THEY sat on the top tier of the amphitheatre at sundown, watching the twin peaks of the Phaedriades change from glowing rose to coral, from softest pink to blue, and finally to the deep translucent violet which shed its mystery over the valley and the shrine, and across the grim encircling heights.

A silence hung between them, comfortable, free from strain, yet the rift, ever-present, hung between them, too, menacing, destructive.

At length Nickolas said it was time to go, speaking softly, with that hint of apology which had puzzled Marika from the very moment of their marriage.

She turned, her wide eyes pensive, and faintly smiling.

'I could stay . . . and stay. . . .'

But Nickolas rose, extending a hand to her, and after leaving the theatre they wandered through the ruins and along the Sacred Way. On a distant ridge a shepherd and his flock were outlined against the darkening sky and Parnassus became bathed in a dun grey light as the sun made its swift descent. Now and then an eagle swooped, casting its eerie shadow along the ground or on to the side of the ravine.

Autumn had come to Delphi, and although a few visitors still frequented the hotels and cafés, the village street no longer echoed with laughter and music until the early hours of the morning, and the coaches had ceased to disgorge their tourists by the hundred. The days, though sunny, were short and often chill; the nights were cold and long.

'Is it very bleak in the winter?' asked Marika as they walked through the village.

'Bleak, and desolate, but it has a special charm which I feel sure will appeal to you.'

After dinner they sat reading as usual, by a roaring fire in the cosy sitting-room. On a side table Nickolas had set out drinks, and some special Turkish confections which Marika liked. Had she not been sure of his feelings for Hilary she could almost have believed he'd been trying to woo her during these past few weeks. But only a few days ago he had gone to Corfu, where Hilary now lived. Marika had begged him to take her with him, but he'd given her a very definite no for an answer. She had lain awake that night, imagining all sorts of things that only served to increase her misery.

She eyed the table but ignored its contents and, becoming restless, dropped her book on to her lap.

'Nickolas, couldn't Souphoula come to us while she's off colour, instead of Pitsa staying there?'

He lowered his book, a quizzical smile touching his lips.

'What's the matter? Are you afraid of being alone with your husband? You can always call on Anna for help should the need arise.'

Marika smiled then.

'It isn't that,' was the confident rejoinder. 'But it's so quiet with everyone gone.'

'Pitsa will be gone altogether in a couple of weeks,' he reminded her. 'So you will, I'm afraid, be limited to my rather inadequate company.'

'Can Souphoula come?' she repeated, ignoring his comment, but Nickolas shook his head.

'Souphoula won't live here, even for a short while, you know that. She loves her own home and will stay there till the end. When Pitsa goes we shall have to get Souphoula some help in from the village.'

'I can do everything,' Marika put in quickly. 'I shall enjoy that.'

'I do not wish you to do the menial tasks,' he said

firmly. 'You will go as usual, and perhaps prepare her tea as Pitsa does now, but the cleaning will be done by a woman from the village.'

'I've nothing to do, Nickolas. It gets monotonous.' She knew her voice held a note of complaint, but though she felt ashamed, she could not bring herself to apologize.

'I shall not be working very much during the winter,' said Nickolas in a distinctly eager voice, but as this failed to bring the desired response he added, with a faint sigh, 'You miss Stephanos, don't you?'

'Terribly.' Her eyes clouded. 'I didn't realize at the time just how much Pitsa and I did for him. He kept us quite busy – reading to him and preparing his meals, and – and every day at the end we talked in Greek for part of the time—' She looked across at Nickolas, tears on her lashes. 'It was supposed to be for half an hour, but I always ran out of words.'

Nickolas stared into the flames, absently flicking the pages of his book. When at last he spoke it seemed to be with difficulty.

'You must regret our marriage – in view of what happened.'

Marika's face took on a brooding expression. She saw herself, running in to Stephanos to show him her dress ... finding him in a coma. Then the doctor, speaking to Nickolas privately ... and, later, Nickolas so pale and grim at the wedding.

She sighed and shook her head.

'We weren't to know he wouldn't ever regain consciousness. What else could we do under the circumstances?' Her glance held neither rancour nor regret. 'Father's happiness was all that mattered to us both at the time.' She smiled at him but, avoiding her glance, he rose abruptly and poured out the drinks. Handing her the glass he said, in a tone of unfamiliar hardness,

'What shall we drink to? What is it that you want

most?'

'I don't know,' she replied helplessly after a long deliberation. 'I do not know, Nickolas.'

'You do know.' His voice became harsh. 'You'd give anything to be away from here, from me! – to be back in England with – with—' He drank deeply and refilled his glass. So unlike him, she mused, for he drank very little. 'Come,' he said, draining the second glass, 'let us go out!'

They went along to the Pavilion and sat on the balcony drinking beer and *ouzo*. Nickolas's air of icy detachment was so pronounced and so frightening that Marika, straining to peer down the vertical drop to the blackness of the chasm below, felt herself truly poised on the edge of a precipice. The rocks, naked and grim, were no more terrible than her fear of Nickolas in this mood.

The following day he handed her a letter from David, watching her as she read it. It contained little of interest, but several times David referred to Nickolas as 'old Nick', 'Pluto' and even 'Hades'. This brought a flush to her cheeks, and Nickolas's eyes narrowed. He was not to know that her heightened colour resulted from anger.

'May I read it?' he asked stiffly as she was about to return it to its envelope.

Had he read it he'd have discovered at once that there was nothing more than friendship between her and David, and, suddenly, she wished him to know it. But those unflattering allusions made it impossible for her to let him read the letter. Her flush deepened as she said,

'No, Nickolas, you can't. I'm sorry.'

There was an instant's frigid silence, then Nickolas spoke in arrogant, inexorable tones.

'In that case, I prefer you to finish with him. You will not write to him again. The affair between you ended on your marriage!'

Marika stiffened; his visit to Corfu was still an open wound.

'I shall please myself. You cannot dictate to me, Nickolas.' She knew immediately she should have controlled her tongue, and felt no surprise when he returned harshly,

'In Greece a woman obeys her husband. I forbid you to reply to his letter!'

The next moment she watched from the window as he strode across the garden to the office. She saw him enter, close the door firmly behind him, and with a sigh of desolation she went upstairs to fetch her coat.

Would she and Nickolas ever make anything of their marriage? she wondered, as she walked slowly in the direction of Souphoula's cottage. Stephanos had been convinced that Nickolas would finish with Hilary, but Stephanos had been wrong. Marika supposed she'd something to be thankful for in Hilary's leaving the house. She felt sure Stephanos had been responsible, but now that he had gone there was the nagging anxiety that Nickolas would persuade her to return.

Remembering the old man's disjointed mumblings about Hilary's owning half the house, Marika wondered that she had left at all. So much activity had occurred at the time. Nickolas seemed to be for ever coming and going; Hilary had been furiously angry – which, thought Marika, was only natural, seeing that Nickolas was having to marry someone else – and finally, Souphoula, of all people, had also been concerned in the proceedings for, to both Pitsa's and Marika's astonishment, she had been taken into Athens, and had stayed overnight.

On Souphoula's return all activity ceased; Hilary had packed her things and left without more ado. From what Souphoula had later said, she now lived at the hotel in Corfu – the hotel to which Nickolas had gone only a few days previously.

Souphoula was much improved, and Marika felt an overwhelming relief on seeing her sitting upright in her usual hard-backed chair. Souphoula's eyes flickered as she examined Marika's face, and after a moment she asked her what was wrong.

'Nothing; I'm fine. Where's Pitsa?'

'Gone into the village to get some provisions. I shall miss the child.'

'I'll come,' promised Marika with a smile. 'And I daresay Pitsa will visit us quite often.'

'Pitsa will be busy rearing children,' returned Souphoula. 'That is the Greek woman's destiny.'

Marika frowned.

'I hope she won't have a baby every year!' she retorted with some heat. 'Pitsa deserves a better life than that.'

The old woman smiled, her lips quivering slightly.

'In England I suppose it is not the thing. Here we expect it. Does Nick know your views on the matter?'

'We haven't – discussed it,' she stammered, going red. Did Souphoula think their marriage was normal? It certainly seemed like it.

Pitsa returned with the groceries and the two girls spent the rest of the afternoon discussing the wedding. Pitsa had grown very lovely during the past weeks, and her figure had always been slender and straight. Marika began to think of the black-robed women of the village, with their high stomachs and sagging breasts, their figures shapeless from years of childbearing, and a sudden depression swept over her at the idea of Pitsa's becoming like that.

But her spirits rose when, later, Pitsa, with tremendous pride in her voice, announced that Kostos had flatly refused to accept a dowry from Nickolas. Pitsa could bring the contents of her bottom drawer, but nothing else.

'Normally the man does the girl a favour by marrying her,' Pitsa went on, in the same tones of pride. 'And so he expects the girl will bring *prika*. It is still quite the thing for the girl to provide the home and everything in it. So I am lucky that Kostos marries me for love. I think that all our lives we shall have of the great happiness – just like you and Nickolas, Marika!'

Marika would have liked to stay for tea, but she knew that Souphoula, with her uncanny perception, would look askance at the mention of such a thing, seeing that Nickolas would then have to take his tea alone.

His manner was frigid during the whole of the evening – still dwelling on her refusal to show him David's letter, she supposed. And because of his coldness she left him early and sat curled up on her bed reading for a long while before getting undressed. Ready to get into bed, she made to turn the key, as usual, but the next minute she stood blinking at the empty keyhole. Glancing over the carpet, she then opened the door and looked on the floor outside. She shrugged, closing the door again. Anna must have removed it in a moment of absent-mindedness; it was too late to trouble her now.

About to get into bed, she suddenly became taut as she heard the sound outside her door. It was opened quietly and Nickolas entered, closing it behind him. Walking calmly into the room, he stood by the dressing-table, one hand in the pocket of his dressing-gown, the other fingering the girdle, with that same peculiar tactility with which the Greek men handled their worry beads. The action both fascinated and terrified her; she took a faltering step backwards, her eyes moving to the dressing-gown she had flung over the back of a chair. With a cool, deliberate gesture, Nickolas picked it up and threw it on to the bed, out of her reach.

The action spoke volumes. Marika's eyes darkened with rapid comprehension as they moved from his sinister, almost evil countenance to the door, and back again.

Her throat felt parched but she managed to say, though quiveringly,

'Why have you come? You c-can't stay. ...'

His manner changed to one of faint amusement as his brows were slowly raised.

'Why have I come? I'm your husband, Marika. We were married, remember?'

Marika contrived to remain calm as she reminded him, gently, that theirs was not a normal marriage.

'That will shortly be rectified, my dear.'

'No, I didn't mean that! I meant I was forced into it – and therefore you can't expect it to be normal. You said yourself that if you forced me into marriage—'

'But I did not force you—'

'Oh, yes, you did, Nickolas. Surely you won't deny that.' He was fingering the girdle again; she could not take her eyes away. If he stayed with her simply for convenience, for lust, she would never forgive him; it would be the end of the marriage. She'd leave him, return to England at once.

'On the contrary, you married me willingly. I seem to remember your being very definite about stressing that point.'

'It was because of Father, you know it was.' Her tones were persuasive, and at the same time reproachful. She appealed to his better nature, realizing that she was fighting for their future, realizing to her own amazement that at the back of her mind dwelt the hope of his one day finishing altogether with Hilary, and they could then try to make something of their marriage.

'Perhaps, but that does not alter the fact that you married me willingly.'

'You're splitting hairs,' she said desperately, her face drained of colour. 'Maybe I did marry you willingly, but it wasn't – it wasn't of my own free will.'

His dark brows rose even higher.

'Who's splitting hairs now?' he inquired, clearly amused, and she stared at him, hoping for some sign of relenting. But, despite his amusement, the inflexibility remained.

'Nickolas,' she said softly, extending her hands in a gesture of entreaty, 'I did it for Father, for your father — we both did it for his sake.'

'Did we?' A sudden, terrible bitterness entered his voice and Marika's eyes flew to his. Something here she did not understand — something unfathomable in that dark and brooding countenance.

'You know it,' she whispered. 'You know very well we did it for his happiness and peace of mind.'

He stood gazing down at her in an attitude of ... could it be indecision? Marika had the strange conviction that he longed to tell her something, but though she waited, he appeared to change his mind. And it seemed to her that his very silence became a threat, for he resumed his adamant, unrelenting manner, and his eyes hardened like points of steel. In almost helpless desperation she made one final effort.

'Nickolas, I don't want you to stay. I don't know — know anything about. ....' She tailed off, the colour rising as she noticed his expression.

'You will learn quickly enough.'

Sick with apprehension, she whispered hoarsely,

'You must go; I can't be a wife to you without ... love!' Even as she spoke she took another step backwards, for her words had unleashed a wrath so violent that she feared for a moment he would strike her.

'I suppose it would be very different if it were your friend David standing here!' he almost snarled, his face darker and more sinister than she had ever seen it. Moving across the room, he wrenched open the door. Her eyes dilated; she spoke without thinking, so great her relief.

'Thank you, Nickolas.'

'Save your breath!' he flung at her. 'I'm not leaving out of any instinct of chivalry or pity. It so happens I am in no mood to deal with a fit of hysterics, which I assume you would immediately indulge in — but don't be too confident; I might be in a very different mood the next time!'

She stared at the closed door, too weak and drained to move. The next time, he had said. For tonight she'd escaped, but there would be other nights – nights when he would not leave. . . .

At last she got into bed, shivering violently until, after the tears had brought some slight relief, she fell into a fitful, troubled slumber.

It was a week later that she told Nickolas she wanted to go home. The nightly strain of sitting on her bed, afraid and taut, waiting for Nickolas to come up, for the silence that told her he'd gone to bed, had proved too much. The nervous tension had even made her bodily ill, for she could neither eat nor sleep.

'If you go home you'll not come back. No, Marika, you're my wife, and your place is here, with me.'

'I will come back, I promise. But please let me go for a little while, just for a visit. Please, Nickolas!'

'You are not going to England,' he said quietly. 'So you can put the idea right out of your head.'

Sudden hatred blazed. The fare – two hundred pounds – prevented her from getting away from this man.

'What good is it doing you to keep me here! I know marriage is for ever; I know I must come back to you – but let me go. I must go home—' She put her hands to her eyes to stem the tears. 'You don't understand,' she said in a quieter tone. And she dropped her hands, looking at him earnestly. 'You don't understand why I must go home, Nickolas.'

'Not understand? What sort of a fool do you take me for? Of course I know why you wish to return to England! And then, from the safety of your country, you'll inform me that you are not coming back. No,' he said firmly, 'you remain here with me.'

Neither argument nor pleading would move him,

though she persevered for a long while until at last, defeated, she went upstairs and kept to her room for the rest of the day. He came up at dinner time. She sat on the bed, her eyes dark and intense, her cheeks damp. She had been sobbing bitterly, and now and then a sob still escaped her. He stood by the door, looking down at her for a long moment; she did not move, nor even raise her head.

'Come down to dinner, Marika,' he said gently. 'It is getting cold.'

'If that is an order, I'll come. If not, I prefer to stay here.'

Nickolas sighed deeply, asking her again to have her dinner with him. She looked up then, bewildered, for there was a strange humility in his tone, and a hint of pleading.

'I don't feel like any dinner.'

'Perhaps you will if you come down.'

'If you don't mind, I'd rather not.'

'Very well!' he snapped, and strode from the room.

When, later, he returned, she was crying again.

'What are all these tears for?' He sounded slightly impatient, and she retorted peevishly,

'I want to go home! You know very well why I'm crying!'

She thought he would never speak, he remained silent for so long, but at last he said in tones of bitter resignation,

'Don't cry any more. You can go home.'

Nickolas would not take her into Athens; he ordered a taxi from the village instead. Half an hour before it was due to arrive Marika said she was going to say good-bye to Souphoula.

'I have plenty of time?'

'You have time, but not plenty. Be as quick as you can.'

Souphoula looked very gaunt and sinister, with her

black eyes scarcely moving and her swollen hands clasped together on her lap.

'So you are really in earnest? I hoped you would change your mind.' Never before had she spoken in those tones, so cold and harsh. Yet her mouth began to soften as she noted the pallor on Marika's face and the dark smudges beneath her eyes. 'Are you coming back?'

'Of course; I must come back.' At first she'd had her doubts. Her promise to Nickolas was vague, yet not deliberately misleading. But now she knew for sure that she'd return. Whatever his feelings for her, he exerted an influence from which she would never escape.

'I wonder ...?' Souphoula stretched out a hand. 'Come here! What have we done to frighten you away?'

Slowly Marika crossed the room. Souphoula's hand was icy cold.

'I'm not being frightened away. I told you, I'm going to England on a visit.'

'I'm no fool, Marika! This is too sudden— Is it Nick's lovemaking? Is he too rough for your English sensibilities?'

'*Souphoula!*'

'No need for embarrassment; in Greece we speak out. Well, child, answer me,' and, when Marika shook her head. 'If you do not tell me what he does, how can I say whether or not you have a complaint?'

'He doesn't do anything – that is, we haven't ever ...' Impossible to go on; she glanced away to the ikons on the wall and wondered vaguely what sort of comfort the Greeks derived from kissing them.

'He has never ... taken you?' Souphoula spoke with disbelief, a most odd expression on her face. 'Are you telling me that Nick has never taken you?'

Hot colour flooded Marika's cheeks; she drew her hand away and moved to the other side of the room.

'I don't like to talk about such things, Souphoula.'

'Rubbish! I'm beginning to think some talking

should be done, for there's a deal I cannot understand. At one time I decided you two had fallen in love, at another I decided I'd made a mistake. Finally I concluded Nick must have married you for convenience, but—' She paused as comprehension dawned. 'He married your for a different reason altogether.'

Glancing at her watch, Marika moved impatiently. What was wrong with Souphoula? Pitsa had hinted that she had begun to ramble at times, and apparently she was right.

'He married me,' she reminded Souphoula gently, 'because of Stephanos. Surely you remember that.'

'Sit down,' ordered Souphoula, and Marika obeyed, though she drew the old woman's attention to the time. 'You have plenty of time. Now, do you still love him?'

'Does it matter?'

'If it didn't I wouldn't be asking. Answer me!'

Swallowing hard, Marika murmured,

'Yes, I do love him.'

'And he doesn't know.' She clicked her tongue in anger. 'Why did you not tell him?'

'Because he doesn't love me. He loves Hilary – I told you.'

The black eyes flickered. Souphoula ignored Marika's reply.

'Yes, it is all plain now. What a fool I am – must be coming to my dotage, child. I disappoint myself. Do you really believe he loves that one?'

Marika said yes and was rewarded with an impatient sigh.

'How stupid you are! And your reaction to what you overheard – so typically English. I love your people, Marika, but they are fools! They have not the depth of thought, so act impulsively. At any cost, you must convince poor Nick that you love that boy. What good did it do you? – tell me that!'

Marika stared in puzzlement. So unlike Souphoula to

show such interest in other people's affairs. And all this talk wasted precious time.

'It saved my pride,' she returned, with an effort at patience.

An angry exclamation in Greek escaped Souphoula. Never before had Marika seen her moved by any sort of emotion.

'You'll have an unpleasant few minutes when you explain about that tonight,' she warned, and Marika became really concerned. Surely Souphoula had not already forgotten she intended taking the flight to England?

'I shall not be explaining,' she murmured soothingly. 'I'm going home – I've come to say good-bye.'

The old woman smiled faintly, and with satisfaction. She gazed into the fire for a long while as if carefully choosing her words.

'Nick knew, before he married you, that his father would never regain consciousness.'

For one stunned, incredulous moment Marika stared at Souphoula. The sun had dropped while they had been talking, and the firelight sent shadows leaping, to catch the sunken face in a grotesque, transparent veil.

'Nickolas . . . knew. . . .?' Marika's voice held disbelief, yet her heart leapt with sudden joy. 'He didn't marry me for Father's sake – Souphoula, is this true?'

'The doctor told him.' With a flash of insight Marika saw everything clearly. Nickolas fighting his conscience; believing she loved David, yet unable to tell her the truth. 'A pity you allowed Hilary to trouble you,' went on Souphoula. 'I couldn't ease your mind entirely because Nick did not take me into his confidence until all the fuss over the business.' She began to explain how Nickolas, after his brother's death, had wished to buy Hilary out. Her price being extortionate, he had been obliged to let her remain a partner. Then, after having installed Kostos as manager in the hotel in Athens, and hoping to interest him in Pitsa, Nickolas had discovered that Hilary had designs on him. The only solution was to deceive her into thinking he cared for her himself. 'With Kostos and Pitsa fixed up, he intended finishing with Hilary, but then came the necessity of marrying you. Caution was still imperative, for he knew he must get her out of the house. He also hoped she would be more reasonable, and sell out to him at a fair price.' Souphoula's mouth set in a thin hard line as she paused in thought for a moment. 'Not only had she the whip hand, but she was also a jealous, frustrated woman – for I suspect it was always Nick she really wanted. Her price was out of all proportion. She stripped us bare, so bare that we had to let her take the hotel in Corfu in addition to the money. But it was worth it, for we now have the business back in the family. I think everything is settled; Nick went over to Corfu a couple of weeks back with his solicitor and the hotel was put into her name.'

Suddenly aware of Marika's glance of surprise, a faint smile touched the old woman's lips. 'I may seem poor, but that is because I have little value for the material things of life. Do not concern yourself, child, I can afford it. I was only too happy to help Nick out. He was stupid and proud not to have asked me before, because the money would have come to him eventually, in any case. I don't suppose he'd have buried his pride this time had it not been that he wanted her out of the house – for your sake.'

Marika tried to speak, but the words choked her. Souphoula and Nickolas ... they'd done all that really for her!

And all she had done in return was to hurt Nickolas so terribly. And she had even misconstrued his visit to Corfu!

Crossing the room swiftly, she buried her face in the folds of the old woman's skirt.

'Thank you for telling me all this, Souphoula—' And

she raised her head, adding impulsively, 'I love you very much.'

The response came brusquely and without sentiment.

'Pity you never thought to say that to Nick. It might have saved a deal of trouble!' An insistent hand urged Marika to her feet. 'Be off, child, I'm sure it's not my company you want!'

A slow, radiant smile spread across Marika's face, but before she had time to speak the door was flung open and Pitsa ran in.

'Alexis says that if you do not come at once he won't be able to get there in time,' she gasped, stopping for breath. 'You know how old and shaky his taxi is; Marika, do hurry!'

'I'm not going,' Marika submitted quietly.

'Not going? – to England?' Pitsa stared from Marika to Souphoula in bewilderment. 'Aren't you leaving us, after all?'

That sounded almost as if Pitsa, like Nickolas, thought she would never have returned, but Marika made no comment on it.

'I have changed my mind, Pitsa. I don't want to go to England at present.' And she added softly, 'Not until Nickolas can come with me.'

'Then you'll be here for my wedding? Oh, Marika, you make me happy now! So very much you make me happy!'

Glancing from one radiant face to the other, the old woman gave a tiny sigh, but it held no regrets.

For she was a goddess in her own right, aloof, mysterious. Fearsome, yet possessed of a strange compelling beauty, she had reached that zenith of peace when, bereft of ambition, unplagued by desire, she could gaze serenely down from her high pedestal to view with faint contempt the struggles and the striving of mere mortals.

'You had better go and do something about that taxi,' she murmured at last. 'If I know Alexis he'll be hopping

184

around like a madman by now.'

'Yes,' agreed Pitsa urgently, 'for Nickolas isn't there to pacify him.'

'Nickolas isn't there?'

'He went out soon after you'd gone. He told Anna he'd be back in about an hour.'

Catching Souphoula's dark glance, Marika bit her lip and flushed with sudden guilt. Unable to say good-bye to her, Nickolas had gone off somewhere on his own. Somewhere . . .?

He stood by one of the columns, bare-headed and motionless, part of the awesome grandeur. Behind him the shining rock faces of the Phaedriades soared sky-wards. In the sky itself the stars gleamed brilliantly clear, like gems in sharp relief below a canopy of velvet.

Marika paused, breathless; Nickolas moved as if sens-ing her presence, then once more became motionless, a dark silhouette against the unearthly radiance of the moonlit Sanctuary. She reach him, still breathless, and he turned in swift concern.

'Souphoula . . .?'

'She is quite well,' came the gentle assurance. 'I've been speaking to her all this time.'

'You realize you've missed your plane.' Nickolas moved away from her, his tones hard and brittle.

'Souphoula told me everything . . . and that you never loved Hilary. I now know why you married me.'

'Hilary?' He turned his head and frowned. 'I – love Hilary? What are you talking about?'

'I thought you loved her—' Marika paused before adding, in a rather frightened tone, 'So I pretended to be in love with David.' Steeling herself for the 'un-pleasant few minutes' of which Souphoula had warned her, Marika was totally unprepared for the violence of his sudden outburst.

'You— You *pretended* to be in love with him! Are you telling me you never loved him?'

'Yes – I was jealous of Hilary—'

'You fool!' he exclaimed savagely. He took a stride towards her, grasped her shoulders and jerked her round to face him. 'Do you know what you escaped? – what we both escaped?' She felt the strength of his fingers, saw the smouldering eyes above her. 'Your refusal to show me the letter incensed me with the desire to teach you that you were mine – mine and not his! That was no gentle lover who came to you – you'd scorned my love, even rejected my friendship, so I came as an enemy, a merciless, avenging enemy—' A shudder swept through him, the shudder of a man who'd escaped some terrible catastrophe. 'Had I remained there would have been no hope of happiness for us. You'd have stayed with me, yes, I'd have forced you, but as my possession, not as my partner.'

Marika swayed slightly and the colour left her face. She forgot the pain of his grip in her overwhelming thankfulness that she had uttered those words which had released his savage fury. For Souphoula was right when she stated that Nickolas was dangerous only when his anger was suppressed.

'There is so much to explain,' she began in faltering tones. 'I realize now that I've been very foolish.'

'Foolish!' he retorted scathingly. 'I felt sure, on our holiday, that you cared— What feminine caprice caused you to practise that kind of deception on me?'

'I was jealous of Hilary,' she explained once more. 'I wanted to save my pride.'

Nickolas uttered a sharp, angry exclamation, though the pressure of his hands relaxed and she sensed also a slight softening of the lines round his mouth. But there was nothing soft in his voice as he exclaimed.

'So because of your stupid pride we've both suffered weeks of unhappiness! Do you know what you deserve?'

Marika swallowed something hard in her throat. Although abashed, she recalled that he, too, had resorted

186

to deception in order to save his pride. But she did not remind him of the incident. Instead she said in a small contrite voice,

'I'm sorry for hurting you, Nickolas,' and waited in breathless expectancy for his response. A long silence ensued. Would he not speak to her? She clasped her hands together, still waiting, rather anxiously, and vaguely aware of a shadowing moon and a distant roll of thunder. She started to say again that there was much that they needed to explain to each other, but he cut her short.

'Then perhaps *you* will begin,' he invited grimly.

'I don't want to talk about that now.' Her voice was edged with tears as she added, tilting back her head to look deeply into his eyes, 'I just want us to – to make harmony. . . .'

He softened instantly; she saw it in his eyes, felt it in the tender caress of his hands. And he bent his dark head to kiss her, with infinite gentleness at first, then with increasing fervour as the pent-up desires of the past weeks became released.

After a long while, and many tender murmurings between them, Marika freed her arms and flung them round his neck, looking up at him with ardent, loving eyes and recalling how, on their first meeting, she had fearfully likened him to a Greek god, sculptured in stone. Nestling her head against him, she felt his warm heart beating, thrilled to the tender strength of his arms about her, and sensed the ardour temporarily controlled. A marble god indeed . . . !

'My little one,' he whispered tenderly, 'we must go – otherwise we shall be caught in a storm.'

He had not yet told her he loved her, and after a shy and timid hesitation she murmured softly,

'If the Oracle were not silent – if it could speak now, I would ask it . . . I would ask it why Nickolas married me, knowing it was unnecessary.' His arms tightened lovingly, but he merely smiled in some amusement at

187

her wife. 'I wonder what the Oracle would reply?' she added on a low insistent note, and when he still made no response her wide eyes searched his face, confident, but with an urgent question.

'The Oracle would say, my darling, that Nickolas married you because he loved you.' He spoke with tender humour yet with a certain reverence, too. 'He loved you then, he loves you now, and he'll love you for ever. That is what the Oracle would reply.'

As he held her, very close, Marika knew again that heady sensation of being poised in a distant, unreal world where time had no existence. The sensation, although exhilarating, was faintly disturbing, too, and she felt a profound relief on hearing the thunder echo warningly through the towering ragged heights.

'Let's go home,' she whispered huskily as a deep silence reigned once more.

She tucked her arm through his, and they made their way from the temple, past the sites of ancient treasuries, past the bases of votive offerings, along the Sacred Way to the Kastalian Spring. Overhead the clouds gathered, ominous and dark, and a faint breeze stirred the vast stillness, like the contented sigh of a god in slumber.

Mills & Boon
Best Seller Romances

The very best of Mills & Boon
brought back for those of you
who missed reading them when they
were first published.
There are three other Best Seller Romances
for you to collect this month.

THE TOWER OF THE WINDS
by Elizabeth Hunter

When her sister died, Charity was determined to take care of
her baby son — but the child's uncle, the masterful Greek
Loukos Papandreous, was equally determined that the baby
was going to remain in Greece — with him. How could Charity
cope with this man who insisted that, as she was a woman,
her opinions were of no account — yet who made her more
and more glad she was a woman?

MAN IN A MILLION
by Roberta Leigh

Harriet wrote a best-seller and was given the chance of producing it as a million-dollar movie. But Joel Blake, the owner
of the studio, believed that women were unfitted for such
work and made his opinion plain. Did it really matter to
Harriet what he thought? As time went by it appeared that
it did?

TENDER IS THE TYRANT
by Violet Winspear

'I — I sensed something *ruthless* about him. He moulds people
to his tastes, and he makes them submit whether they want
to or not,' Lauri described Maxim di Corte to her aunt Pat
when, as an inexperienced girl, Lauri first joined Maxim's
famous ballet company. There was no doubt that Maxim di
Corte would use these ruthless qualities to make her submit
to him as a dancer, but could be make her do the same for
him — as a woman?

Mills & Boon
Best Seller Romances

The very best of Mills & Boon Romances
brought back for those of you who missed
them when they were first published.
In October
we bring back the following four
great romantic titles.

THE AUTOCRAT OF MELHURST
by Anne Hampson

Claire had promised Simon Condliffe that she would stay on
in her job as nanny to his small niece as long as he needed her
— but she hadn't bargained on falling in love with him, and
then having to watch him with his close friend — or was she
his fiancée? — Ursula Corwell.

LORD OF ZARACUS
by Anne Mather

When Carolyn joined her archaeologist father in Mexico, she
found herself immediately in conflict with Don Carlos, who
owned the valley where her father was searching for a Zapotec
city. Don Carlos thought she was 'a typical product of the
permissive society' and Carolyn let him know that 'I am not
one of your peons'. It seemed an inauspicious beginning to
their relationship. And yet—

LOGAN'S ISLAND
by Mary Wibberley

Helen had inherited an island off the coast of Brazil — jointly
with an unknown man called Jake Logan. Its name — Island
of Storms — just about summed up the wildly antagonistic
relationship that promptly developed between the two of
them!

LOVE'S PRISONER
by Violet Winspear

Meeting Lafe Sheridan proved a milestone in Eden's young
life, and she knew that no man would ever mean as much to
her. But her beautiful sister had more effect on him . . . He
was rich and lonely, and Gale had always meant to marry a
rich man . . .

If you have difficulty in obtaining any of these books through
your local paperback retailer, write to:

Mills & Boon Reader Service
P.O. Box 236, Thornton Road, Croydon, Surrey, CR9 3RU.